FISHKE
THE LAME

by
MENDELE MOCHER SEFORIM

Translated from the Yiddish by
GERALD STILLMAN

Drawings by
AHRON GELLES

THOMAS YOSELOFF
NEW YORK · LONDON

© 1960 BY SAGAMORE PRESS, INC.
LIBRARY OF CONGRESS CATALOG CARD NUMBER: 60-6836

THOMAS YOSELOFF, *PUBLISHER*
11 EAST 36TH STREET
NEW YORK 16, N. Y.

THOMAS YOSELOFF LTD.
123 NEW BOND STREET
LONDON W. 1, ENGLAND

PRINTED IN THE UNITED STATES OF AMERICA

FISHKE THE LAME

INTRODUCTION

I

Fishke the Lame IS A BOOK ABOUT BEGGARS AND TRAMPS. Mendele Mocher Seforim deals here with the "lower depths" of Jewish life in the Pale of Settlement of Tsarist Russia. ". . . It has been my lot to descend to the depths, to the cellars of our Jewish life. My stock in trade is rags and moldy wares. My dealings are with paupers and beggars, the poor wretches of life . . . the dregs of humanity . . ." Thus wrote Mendele to his friend Menasha Margolius.

Unfortunately, large numbers of Jews found themselves in the cellars of Jewish life. Aside from the very wealthy, few indeed were the Jews who could predict where tomorrow's meal would come from. The only predictable thing about life for them was its instability, its insecurity and the ever-present threat of hunger and disease. In *The Jews in Russia*, published in 1872, I. Orshansky described the plight of the Jews in White Russia and Polesye:

. . . Half, if not three-quarters, of the Jewish population consists of individuals who could be classified as go-betweens and middlemen, as vagrants and loiterers—not because these characteristics stem from laziness or lack of desire to work, but rather because these wretched people whose sole concern is to obtain a crust of bread live in torment from day to day, not having the slightest means or opportunity to find gainful em-

3

ployment in productive work. . . . These unfortunate families own nothing, live in filth and poverty, not knowing how or whether they will eat on the following day. Sheer necessity forces them to employ irregular means to provide themselves with the barest essentials of life . . .

In Berditchev [this is the city which Mendele refers to as Glupsk in all his works—G.S.] there are as yet no welfare laws concerning the poverty-stricken and unsanitary conditions of the Jews. Some 5000 families, about 25,000 souls, live from day to day only on what the Lord provides. They live in extremely crowded conditions. It very often happens that several families occupy one or two rooms in a ruined hovel, so that at night there is no free floor space between the sleepers . . .[1]

Restricted to living within the Pale of Settlement and even there excluded from many cities, barred from joining merchant and artisan guilds, prohibited from buying land, the economic base of Jewish life was bound to be warped and crippled. With so many avenues of normal employment sealed off to them, the necessities of life forced great numbers of Jews to catch as catch can, to become *luftmenschen*—to make a living from thin air, so to speak. Mendele's traveling companion, Reb Alter, sums the situation up in a nutshell in *Fishke*:

"As far as I'm concerned, you can cut the whole story short. All of Israel—one big pauper! And an end to this nonsense . . ."

The pauperized state of the mass of Jews is a subject of predominating concern for Mendele in almost all his works. His pen flashes with angry bolts of lightning, with salty tears of frustration, with biting irony—as the occa-

[1] Quoted by M. Wiener, *History of Yiddish Literature in the XIX Century*, Vol. II, New York, 1946.

4

sion demands—when dealing with this subject. In *The Travels of Benjamin III*, there is a delightful passage which conveys the utter pointlessness and hopelessness of Jewish occupations, couched in terms of that humor so characteristic of the best in Yiddish writing, which allows the unbearable to be borne:

. . . Ask a Jew of Tuneyadevkeh how he makes a living. His first reaction is to stand there paralyzed. The poor man is befuddled and doesn't know what to say. A little later, he revives and begins to explain:

"Who, me? How I make a living? Me? *Ett,* there is a God, I tell you here and now, who does not forsake any of his creatures. He has provided before and will probably provide some more, I tell you right here and now."

"Still, what do you do? Do you at least have a trade or a craft?"

"Praise the Lord! I have, thank God, as you see me right here and now, a gift from His Blessed Name, an instrument, a musical voice, and I also recite the supplemental prayers during the Solemn Days. Occasionally I am a *Mohel,* and before Passover I knead dough for making *matzos*—there isn't another kneader like me in the world, I tell you right here and now! Sometimes, I manage to make a match, I do. Also, this is between me and you, I have an interest in a tavern which can be milked a little. I have a goat which can be milked a lot, may the Evil Eye not harm her, and not far from here, I have a rich relative who can also, when times are bad, be milked a little. Now, aside from all these things, I tell you right here and now, God is a father and the children of Israel are both merciful and generous, I tell you right here and now . . ."

Even worse than the oppression of the mass of Jews by the discriminatory legislation of the Russian government was their merciless exploitation by their own upper class

Fishke, like Mendele's other novels, has a substantial moralistic lining.

In order to convey his various messages as distinctly as possible, Mendele develops his characters by means of their reactions to external circumstances. The character is seen in the light of how the outside world affects him and makes him act and think. He is tossed about and buffeted by a seemingly wanton and heartless fate. No sooner do the rays of hope break through the clouds of one misfortune when he is engulfed by an even greater misfortune until justice and righteousness triumph at last. Peril and mystery lurk behind each page and the character grows by means of his reactions to them.

Although many of the characters in *Fishke* are either good or evil, Mendele reaches greatness with his three-dimensional portrayals of the characters of Fishke, Reb Alter and of Mendele himself. These personages have both virtues and weaknesses, bravery and cowardice, altruism and selfishness.

Mendele's great message in *Fishke* is that it is the exploitation and oppression of people that is despicable and not the people themselves. Poverty is hateful, but the poor are not. To this end, he describes the ugly and repulsive sides of the beggar's life with frank realism. He makes no attempt to prettify or omit details. One gets the impression that he is sometimes deliberately coarse. But then he proceeds to show how human love and warmth can flourish in even so barren a soil. He portrays the spiritual goodness and beauty that can reside in the physically ugly and thereby accomplishes his goal.

Mendele's writing is pervaded with a humanism, a sincere love for people, that makes his moralizing easy to take. He has a fatherly, not patronizing, attitude toward his people. He wants them to improve their ways, to escape from the medieval morass in which they are wallowing, to catch up with modern times. He shows them their faults and then, for contrast, points out the attributes he would so dearly like to see them have.

His humanism is accompanied by and nourished by that rich Jewish humor which invariably evokes a response from the reader, varying from a chuckle to a roar. It is a humor based on making capital of one's own weaknesses. It is the antithesis of pomposity. It cannot take the hardships and tribulations imposed by life with utter seriousness. It shrugs them off by illuminating their ludicrous aspects. It is a humor turned back on itself which makes an almost unbearable life bearable.

Mendele is a past master at this type of humor and has no equal in Yiddish literature in its application with the exception of Sholom Aleichem. That *Fishke* is full of this humor from beginning to end can be seen directly by reading the first and last sentences of the novel.

Another aspect of Mendele's humanism is his sensitivity to natural beauty. He never sees nature apart from man. His trees whisper to each other and tickle each other with their branches; his birds hop up and down in song like the cantor in a synagogue; his stalks of grain wave their heads in the wind and tell each other secrets like little children. God, Man and Nature are One. This sensitivity to nature received its first impetus at his stepfather's home in Melniki, a place of rare natural beauty where he lived for several months. He describes its effect on him in these terms:

It was in this remote and isolated spot that my Muse first revealed herself to me. . . . With all her magic charms, she drew

9

me after her into the woods, under a green tree where all was peace and quiet. She drew me into a bond with the trees of the forest, the birds in the sky and the animals on the ground, and she taught me their language. . . .[2]

It is Mendele's warm humanism and humor which make *Fishke* such a delightfully entertaining work to read despite some of its antique characteristics.

III

Much of Mendele's knowledge of the wandering life of the beggars and tramps was a result of first-hand experience. When he was about seventeen years old, he was studying in his native town of Kapulya and living alone. His father had died several years earlier and his mother had remarried and moved to the nearby town of Melniki. A well-known tramp by the name of Avreml the Limper returned to Kapulya at this time with a stock of wonderful tales about the fortunes to be had in the Volhynia and the south of Russia. It was there that "milk and honey flowed in the streets." These tales fired the imagination of the impressionable seventeen-year-old Mendele and he left with Avreml for the wide-open spaces. They wandered through Lithuania and then the whole southwestern portion of Russia—through the Volhynia, Podolya and the Ukraine. They slept in poorhouses or on the benches in Houses of Study along the way. They begged from door to door across the length and breadth of the Jewish Pale of Settlement. The travels in the broken-down wagon pulled by an emaciated old mare laid the foundation for Mendele Mocher Seforim's van of books and wares and his wise, but perpetually hungry, old nag. This

[2] Zalman Reisin, *Lexicon of Yiddish Literature*, Vol. I, Vilna, 1926.

period of wandering gave Mendele the background material for this novel as well as his chief protagonist Fishke for whom, it has been said,[3] Avreml the Limper was the prototype.

The first version of *Fishke the Lame*, a forty-five page booklet, appeared in the Ukrainian city of Zhitomir in 1869, some sixteen years after Mendele's journeys with Avreml. A second version was completed in 1876 but never published. The third version grew into the present book and was issued in 1888. There was yet a fourth version in Hebrew which Mendele retitled *The Beggar Book*. It is the third version, in the edition released by the printing house "Yiddish Buch" in Warsaw in 1953 under the editorship of David Sfard, upon which this translation is based.

Gerald Stillman

Nutley, N.J.

[3] Z. Reisin, *ibid.*

To my dear, beloved friend
Menasha Margolius
I dedicate this book from the depths of my heart.

Dear friend,

Sad is my melody in the symphony of Yiddish literature. My works express the very core of a Jew who, even when he does sing a merry tune, sounds from afar as if he were sobbing and weeping. Why, even his festive *Shabbes* hymns sound as if they were taken out of the Book of Lamentations. When he laughs, there are tears in his eyes. When he tries to make merry, bitter sighs escape from the depths of his heart—it's always *oy-vay,* woe is me, *vay!*

I am not, God forbid, trying to give myself airs by saying that I am a nightingale in Yiddish literature, although, in one respect, there is a great deal of similarity between me and him. This melancholy poet of the birds pours out his sad heart and sings his dirgelike melodies precisely in springtime when all the world is newborn, when the buds burst into bloom, when delicious aromas tickle the nostrils, when everything looks bright and rosy and one's heart skips a beat for joy.

You and I, my dear friend, both began our work in Yiddish literature in the springtime of Jewish life here in our land. From 1860 onward, a new life seemed to have begun for Jews—a more relaxed life, a life full of hope for the future. At that time, we were both still very young. Each of us seized his pen with zeal and began to work away lustily, each according to his own bent. The people licked their fingers from your writing. They were thoroughly delighted to read the sweet words you wrote about many important matters in Jewish life. You were an advocate of righteousness among Jews and lectured them gently, in friendly fashion, on how to know themselves, to learn how to live and become the equals of other peoples. Pearls fell from your lips, lustrous pearls which shine and will always be an ornament for Yiddish literature.

I, too, hummed a tune in my own way during those happy spring days, but there was always one note which repeated gloomily and cast a spell of melancholy over the listeners. Some of them listened readily, although with heavy hearts; others made faces, scratched themselves unhappily, and were annoyed because I reminded them of unpleasant things and made their ears tingle. Be that as it may, I sang my song the only way I could.

That promising spring has long since passed. Woe, oh woe is to the life of a Jew! Trouble has made me lose my desire to write. It has been a good while since I have lost my tongue.

And if I now take my gaunt and shriveled pen in hand and again attempt to use my voice, it is only thanks to you, you whose company has restored my balance and renewed my strength. Your clever words, your unrelenting labors in behalf of our people have refreshed me and inspired me with the desire to undertake some useful labor also. A spark has risen from the holy fire which ever burns in your Jewish heart and has alighted in my breast where it burst into flame and is now burning with the vigor of my youthful years.

Yes, we both commenced our literary labors at the same time, but our fortunes have not been the same. You scale the great heights. There you deal with the gems and jewels of Jewish history. You put our best foot forward by exhibiting our most sparkling antique diamonds, the best and dearest in the life of our people. You deal with Rabbi Hillel, Rabbi Meir, Rabbi Akiba and other greats —men of the highest renown.

On the other hand, it has been my lot to descend to the depths, to the cellars of our Jewish life. My stock in trade is: rags and moldy wares. My dealings are with paupers and beggars, the poor wretches of life; with degenerates, cripples, charlatans and other unfortunates, the dregs of humanity. I always dream of beggars. Before my eyes, I always see a basket soaring—the old, familiar Jewish beggar basket. No matter which way I turn my eyes, the basket is before me. No matter what I say or do, the basket comes soaring up to me! *Oy*, it's always the basket, the Jewish beggar basket!

Yes, dear friend, through you the fire for writing has revived in me and has again produced a punishment for our numerous iniquities, a basket! A *Fishke der Kroomer** with which I am appearing before the public after such a long period of silence. I know that my *Fishke der Kroomer* is not the most suitable gift with which to express my gratitude for your friendship, but knowing your warm heart and your understanding of people, I dare to hope that you will accept my poor Fishke with a "Welcome!" Possibly, you will invite him into your home and introduce him to your family and friends. Fishke will gladly rest with you for a while, put his basket aside and tell you tales which you will enjoy. With this picture before my eyes, I smile with pleasure and thank you from the depths of my heart,

The Author

* *Fishke the Lame,* the English title of the present work.

15

I

JUST WHEN THE BRIGHT SUN BEGINS TO SHINE PROCLAIM-
ing another summer to the land, when people feel newly
born and their hearts fill with joy at the sight of God's
glorious world—just then the time for wailing and weeping arrives among Jews. This time of sorrow brings with
it a host of mournful days: days of fasting, days of self-
torment, days of grief and tears—starting at the end of
Passover and lasting well into the damp cold and deep
mud of autumn.

This is the very time when I, Mendele the Book Ped-
dler, am busiest. I travel from fair to fair and from town
to town to provide the children of Israel with all the wares
needed for shedding tears: Books of Lamentations, Penitential Prayer Books, women's Books of Supplication,
ram's-horns for the Day of Atonement, and prayer books
for festivals. In short, while Jews weep and wail all
summer long, my business thrives. But that's not the
point . . .

Early one morning on the road, it was the seventeenth
day in the month of *Tammuz,** I sat on my wagon in my
prayer shawl and *tefillin,* my whip in my hand, in an altogether Jewish manner. My eyes were shut to keep the
distracting light of day from interfering with my prayers.
Satan would tempt me, though. Nature, or whatever it is
called, was wondrously beautiful, a sight to behold. I was

* Yiddish words in italics will usually be found in the glossary at
the end of the book.

17

strongly driven, as though by witchcraft, to steal a glimpse. I wrestled with myself for quite a while.

My Good Mentor said, "For shame! You mustn't!"

"It's all right! Enjoy yourself, silly!" prodded my Evil Genius and at the same time forced open one of my eyes.

As if for spite, I was overwhelmed by the exquisite panorama which greeted my eye.

Fields peppered with blooming buckwheat as white as snow were embroidered with stripes of golden-yellow wheat and pale-green stalks of corn; a pleasant valley, the sides of which were covered with groves of nut trees; and below, a brook—clean and clear as crystal—into which the rays of the sun ducked and leaped out again in a shower of blinding golden sparks. In the distance, the cows and sheep at pasture looked like gray and red specks.

"*Feh, feh!* For shame!" my Evil Genius mocked and flung the well-known precept at me: "Should a Jew, while traveling, interrupt his prayers and say, 'How pretty is the tree, how beautiful the field,' he commits a grievous sin." But at the same moment, he blew into my nostrils the delicious fragrance of the stacks of newly cut hay, of herbs and roots—fragrances which trickled into my very extremities; the tricky melodies of the myriad songbirds drifted into my ears and tickled my soul. He sent a soft warm breeze across my face; it rippled through my prayer curls and whispered: "Look, enjoy yourself and be a man, silly Jew that you are!"

I babbled and gabbled, and truth to tell, I myself did not know about what. My thoughts ran away with themselves; curses and sneers pecked at my brain:

"Cadaverous creatures! Neither substance nor soul! Creatures with their souls absorbed in eating! Creatures without taste or smell. Dried out, useless rubbish!"

18

I began to rock back and forth with forced devotion so as to keep my mind from wandering. But I suddenly heard my mouth twist the prayer to say, ". . . he who returns to the dead carrion their souls."

Why? To whom did this refer? I almost jumped, so ashamed did I feel of my ugly thoughts. To smoothe over my error against the One Above, I acted as if I had meant something entirely different: it was this horse of mine. I flicked the good-for-nothing with the whip and growled, "A-a-a-h! You carrion, you!"

This was indeed a clever act, but today it was of little use. Somehow I was deeply concerned that such thoughts should occur to me today of all days—on this day, when we bewail and lament the great misfortune that once befell us children of Israel: the army of Nebuchadnezzar, King of Babylonia had entered Jerusalem and razed it to the ground. Forcing myself to feel contrite, I said the penitential prayer for this day in a tearful voice which mounted in pitch until it reached a climax of sorrow at those bitter words of the refrain:

"And the horned monster, the Tatar from the North, swept me from my feet like a jet of water and carried me far, far away . . ."

Once a Jew has shouted a psalm to his heart's content or talked himself hoarse repeating penitential prayers, he feels greatly relieved and, like a child who has had a good cry after a whipping, is quite happy again. So I felt now, half reclining in my wagon, smoothing my beard, with a beaming countenance as if to say: "Well, my share is done, I've done my duty. And now, *Gottenyu,* the rest is up to You; show Yourself, O Father, Merciful and Just One!"

19

"Come now, come! Forgive me!" I looked at my horse with good will, apologizing in my heart for having called him "carrion" before. My *shlimmazel* kneeled on his front legs, bowed his head to the ground, and groaned as if to say:

"Your lordship! How about something to eat?"

"True! You're as bright as the light of day," I said, signaling that he might rise now, that is, get up on his feet. Not in vain is it stated in the Book of Lamentations: "Zion, even your cattle and poultry are clever . . ." But that's not my point.

This profound thought led to others concerning the children of Israel; I mused about their wisdom, their mode of living, their communal leaders, and their sorry condition. My thoughts strayed hither and thither. Before me I saw the horned monster, Nebuchadnezzar and his army, bloody battles, confusion and commotion. The army tore down walls, smashed out doors and windows. Jews, many with packages of wares and old clothes, cried for help, and mustering their courage—fled. I seized a stick and was about to—when boom! I found myself stretched out flat on my back on the ground.

Apparently, let it not be repeated to others, I had been napping in the midst of my prayers. My wagon, I saw, had gone into a puddle, of the type known in the coachmen's jargon as "an inkwell." The axle hub of another wagon was caught in my rear wheel. My poor horse stood there in agony with one leg over the shaft, all twisted in the harness and puffing like a goose. From the other side of the wagon flowed a stream of deadly curses, in Yiddish, interrupted only by a spell of coughing and choking.

"A Jew," I thought; "then there is no danger." And I strode in anger to the other side of the wagon. There, underneath, lay a Jew smothered in his prayer shawl and *tefillin,* his whip entangled in the leather thongs of his *tefillin,* struggling for all he was worth to free himself.

I shouted, "What do you call this?"

And he: "What do you mean, 'What do you call this'?"

"How does a Jew dare to fall asleep while praying?" I exclaimed.

"How can a Jew snore away like that?" he retorted.

I cursed his father and his entire generation and he— my mother and hers. I whipped his horse and he, freeing himself, ran in a fury to whip mine. Both horses reared on their hind legs. In a frenzy, we flew at each other like two raging cocks and were about to seize each other's prayer curls, when we stopped and stared at each other for a silent moment. It must have looked strange, indeed: two Jewish champions in their prayer shawls and *tefillin,* facing each other in a rage, ready to exhibit their prowess and slap each other, right in the middle of this open field, as though they'd been arguing in a *House of Study,** forgive the comparison! It would really be worth going to some trouble to witness a charming scene like this one. We stood there, ready to slap each other in a moment, when suddenly we both jumped back several paces and, in great surprise, shouted in one voice:

"*Oy,* Reb Alter!"

"*Oy, oy!* Reb Mendele!"

Alter *Yaknehoz* was a powerful little man with a big belly. His face was overgrown with a thick mat of dirty-yellow hair of which there was enough to provide for prayer curls, beard and mustaches not only for himself but for several more Jews as well. In the midst of this sea of hair lay an island—a broad, fleshy nose which, being

* See glossary.

21

with vigor. Several of the peasants, although not children of Israel, but the truth must be told, had the goodness of heart to come and help us in this, our time of need. By dint of their pushing, my wagon was soon out of the "inkwell." Were it not for them, we would have puttered around for God knows how long and would probably have torn our prayer shawls to tatters. But together with the peasants it was an entirely different story: they pushed in real earnest, for the hands were the hands of Esau; but with us it was only the voice, and the voice was the voice of Jacob. We grunted and groaned and struggled as if we were really pushing. . . . But that's not my point.

As soon as the road was cleared, these vulgar louts went their way, turning only to mock and jeer at us for being dressed like orthodox priests, forgive the comparison, and for walking alongside the horses, serving the Creator with whip in hand. Some of them, grasping the lower corner of their coats to form the shape of a "sow's ear," pointed them at us, shouting: "Jewish swine!" Alter was hardly bothered. "Remember whence it comes," he shrugged. "Who is there to get insulted at?" But I was deeply hurt by their mocking. *G'vald*, Father in Heaven, why? Why?

"Almighty God!" I began in the plaintive style of the women's *techinas*. "Ope Thine eyes and do mark, from Thy retreat which is the Heaven above, how Thy dear Name is holden by them, for in awe do they stand of Thy might, and Thy word do they cherish most reverently. Do Thou then cause to descend upon us Thy compassion that we may find Favor and Grace in Thine eyes and in the eyes of all people. Do Thou then shield Thy most surely beloved sheep and let Thy Mercy dwell among Thy constant worshipers. Do Thou also improve my fortune for having this day praised and glorified Thy Name in

24

deep reverence. Cause to descend upon me, Thy slave Mendl, son of Thy maid Gnendl, and upon all of Israel, some good bit of business that our spirits may be at ease, Amen!"

II

WITHOUT FURTHER ADO, WE CLIMBED UP ON OUR WAG-
ons and off we went. My wagon was in front. Behind me
rode Alter in a van with tattered matting, four crooked
wheels with wedges between the spokes and rims tied
together with rope. The greased wheel blocks tossed from
side to side on their axles, creaking and groaning, unable
to find themselves a comfortable position. A tall, strikingly
lean beast put itself to the trouble of drawing this van—
a scrofulous mare with a flea-bitten back full of blisters,
with long ears, a twisted and tangled mane matted with
wisps of hay and wads of cotton padding which were coming out of her collar.

All that remained to be said of my morning prayers
were the last few verses, about which, even under ordinary
circumstances, little fuss is made. Having done with my
prayers, an entirely new contest developed with my Evil
Genius.

"Go ahead," he urged. "Take a sip of brandy! It will re-
fresh your heart."

"*Ai, Ai!*" I wrinkled my nose in refusal. "On the seventeenth of *Tammuz!* On such a day of fasting!"

"*Ett!*" came back a reply. "There's a bit of difference
between a Jew today and one in the times of Nebuchadnezzar! There are bigger troubles today and yet . . .
nothing. Don't be silly. You're old and weak, poor man.
There's no harm in it!"

I swept my hand across my face as if to brush away a

26

troublesome fly and in the meanwhile stole a wee glance at the little satchel back in the wagon—the little satchel where I always kept a good bit of brandy, buckwheat cookies, rye cakes, garlic, onion, and other greens. My mouth watered, my heart grew faint, my stomach growled:

"*G'vald,* help! A drop of brandy! *G'vald,* something to eat!"

I turned my head away swiftly and fixed my attention on the fields about me in an effort to drive away these evil thoughts.

The sky was blue and clear without a trace of cloud. The sun baked and broiled. There was not the slightest breeze, not even a breath of air, for relief. The stalks of grain in the fields, the trees in the woods stood stock still —as though petrified. The cows at pasture lay fatigued, their necks outstretched, wiggling their ears from time to time and chewing their cud. Some dug up the earth with their horns and pushed it underneath them with their hoofs while bellowing from heat. The bull lifted his head and went galloping madly, tossing his head from side to side, stopped suddenly and lowered his brow almost to the ground. He sniffed, blew hard through his nostrils, let out a great bellow and stamped his feet. Near an old, gnarled, half dried-up willow, split in half by a thunderclap long ago, stood a herd of horses, their heads thrown over each other to create some shade; they whisked their tails to and fro to get rid of the troublesome flies. High up in a tree, a magpie swayed back and forth on a branch. It looked, for all the world, as if she wore a little white prayer shawl with the blue stripes in front and was praying with a rocking motion. She bowed her little head in supplication, hopped and chirped a few times . . . then remained still again, without a sound, stretching out

27

her little neck and staring into the world with sleepy little eyes.

All along the road there was only silence, not the slightest sound, not a peep; there was not even a bird in flight; only mosquitoes and midges carried on like demons, flying by with a hum and a hiss, whispering a secret into one's ear and then—gone again. Only in the haystacks, among the stalks, crickets chirped incessantly; they were in full cry.

It was hot. It was quiet, and wondrously beautiful. Hush! God's creatures were resting. . . .

On account of the heat, I sprawled in my wagon in my shirt sleeves, pardon my appearance, and prayer shawl. I had pushed my stitched felt cap to the back of my head and rolled my heavy woolen stockings, from Breslau, down to my ankles—stockings which, in expiation of our manifold sins, I wore even during the summer—and perspired profusely. Because I love to perspire, I would have enjoyed the heat if the sun were not beating directly into my eyes; I could lie for hours on the upper bench in the steam bath in the very greatest heat. My father, his memory be praised, had accustomed me to it even as a child. He was a hot, smoldering, burning, fiery Jew. He loved to steam himself through and through and thereby made a name for himself. He was greatly beloved among the people, for the very gist of Jewishness is to be found in this fiery nature. Therefore they regarded him as a respectable Jew who was close to God. They spoke of him with reverence:

"Oh, yes, as far as whipping goes, he is a deep scholar. He's a past master on the subject 'steam bath.' He knows . . . he knows all there is to know about sweating!"

Sweating is a Jewish thing. Not a Sabbath goes by, not a holiday, when a Jew does not find himself in a good sweat. Who, among all the seventy nations of the world, has sweated more than the Jews? But that's not my point.

And while I lay there sweating, how I did need refreshment! My throat was dry, my lips were parched and crying for a drink, I was dying for some food. My Evil Genius seized upon me again, stronger than ever, and enumerated the whole list of Jewish delicacies:

"Broiled *ledvetsa* with porridge; sweet-and-sour meat; a *lokshn* pudding with a 'thief' (a stuffed neck of chicken hidden within); boiled *farfel*, fried with bits of chicken skin." I became faint; my limbs turned limp. My appetite was ferocious. But he went right on:

"Thin dough stuffed with meat, jellied calves' feet with liver slices; radish and onion; the crop of a tom turkey in a candied parsnip sauce . . ."

And suddenly, I don't know how it happened, the little satchel appeared before me, as if it had sprung out of the earth.

"*Lechayim*, to your health, silly!" the demon spoke through me. "You've been foolish enough for one day, you dolt!"

My hand stretched forth, by itself somehow, opened the satchel and swiftly snatched the bottle. I looked about like a thief when suddenly my horse's eye brought me to a dead halt. In the process of scratching his neck on the shaft, he had turned his head toward the wagon and scowled at me with resentment, as if to say:

"Here, look! My hind leg is all swollen and bandaged with rags; one of my eyes keeps on watering; my neck is chafed; my mouth, a useless organ, has forgotten the taste of oats. Still in all, what can I do? I just drag along, hungry, sick, and wretched—not even thinking of throwing off the yoke, God forbid."

The bottle slid out of my hand, back into its resting place. I pushed the little satchel away from me in great shame, groaning from the depths of my heart:

"So this is what has come to pass! This is who must serve me as an example; from him must I learn wisdom! *Milpani mib'haymess ho'erets*—he teaches us by means of the cattle of the earth. . . . No, horse o'mine! I will not throw off the yoke either. We'll live somehow, Reb Horse, the devil won't take either of us! *Adam ub'haymeh*—man and beast—*toyshiah adonai*—are both helped by the Lord!"

Once a Jew has broken himself of the vile passion of eating, food ceases to be a matter of importance to him and he can spend the rest of his life requiring almost nothing. To this very day, in these modern times, many a Jew can be found who has only the vestige of a stomach— truly, the size of an olive pit. And there are great hopes that with the passing of time—if only the kosher meat tax is retained and the activities of the charity workers and their brethren go unhampered—Jews will drift further and further away from eating until among future generations there will be no trace left of the digestive tract at all, except for piles. Jews will then present a pretty picture to the eyes of the rest of the world. . . .

The point of this discourse is that, having pushed the little satchel away, I somehow felt much stronger. I lay back thinking about business and hummed a sad little tune. Everything appeared to be in order. But the devil had to bring into being a peasant lass, ugly as they come, with a pot of mushrooms, my favorite dish. Any pious man in my position would have taken it for granted that this was the Evil Genius himself, disguised in the form of a female in order to . . . But not I! I had to take a good look. It really was only a simple peasant lass! And asking me to buy the mushrooms together with the pot for only ten groschen, she pushed it right under my nose. I was almost overcome by the aroma. It went to my heart. My mouth watered and I felt faint. Oh God, how I wanted it! Fearing that I would lose control of myself, I jumped off the wagon as if I were running from a fire. It was a sheer miracle that I did not break nape and neck. I shouted with a voice that was not mine: "Reb Alter!" My purpose was that Alter should be my chaperon.

There, in his wagon, my Reb Alter lay flat on his back, both hands under his head, red as a beet: his shirt was open, forgive his appearance, and his woolly red-haired chest exposed, burnt, roasted, and so covered with sweat, oh enemies of Zion, that my heart almost broke to see him thus.

"Wha—a—at?" called Alter without stirring when he heard my cry. "What's the matter?"

A quick glance told me that she of the mushrooms was gone. It was as though she had evaporated. Since I had to say something, I asked Alter:

"Tell me, what time do you think it might be now?"

"What time do I think it might be now?" repeated Alter in a hollow voice. "How should I know? Our eyes will probably pop from their sockets waiting for the first stars to appear. That's certain. My, it's awfully hot!"

"A delicious heat, eh? Are you sweating, Reb Alter?" I asked, walking alongside his wagon. "I think it's time to rest. Our lions are weary, they are barely dragging along. It is still many versts to Glupsk; and then maybe a couple more. Down yonder where the woods start, I see a good spot on the left for the horses to feed. It's not far."

A few minutes later, we turned off the road to the spot where the woods started, among pretty fields and a good green meadow. We unharnessed our lions and let them feed in freedom at the edge of the woods. We lay down under a tree.

III

ALTER YAKNEHOZ BREATHED HEAVILY BECAUSE OF THE
heat. His moans and groans affected me so that my heart
melted with pity. To cheer him up a bit and partly to
make the time pass more quickly, I engaged him in the
following conversation:

"Well, Reb Alter, is it hot enough for you?"

"*Beh!*" Alter answered briefly and somewhat vexed,
as he slid further under the tree in an effort to hide himself from the rays of the sun which cut through the
branches.

"*Feh!* This day of fasting is making me sick! Is that you
groaning like that?" I probed Alter again, having firmly
resolved that though I should die in the attempt I would
get him to speak.

"*Beh!*" Alter answered, and slid still further under the
tree.

I was not disposed to be happy with only a "*Beh!*" for
an answer. "Aha!" I thought. "You hide-bound old mule!
I'll fix you! I'll make you talk. If heat and sweat won't do
it, then the subject will have to be business—the best, in
fact the only topic to make a silent Jew talkative. A Jew,
even if he be on his deathbed, will come alive as soon as
he hears something about business; he comes alive and
even the Angel of Death cannot come near him at that
moment. God help the man who must cross the path of a
rich merchant when he is occupied with business: he will

demolish anyone, even his best friend, his own brother, with his glance . . . But that's not my point."

I turned to Alter and said: "You and I, Reb Alter, are going to do some trading, I think! I'm glad that we met each other today. Oh, I have some stuff with me today that is worth its weight in gold!"

My new tactic had its effect. Alter was a changed man. He raised his head, turned toward me and pricked up his ears. I continued to feed the fire:

"This time, Reb Alter, all our trading will be on a cash basis. You say you're coming from the fair at Yarmelinetz, so your pockets must be bulging with money, may the Evil Eye not harm them."

"Bulging pockets, yes! A heart bulging with trouble is all I have," said Alter testily. "I tell you, Reb Mendl . . . but—nothing . . . an unlucky man would be better off if he hadn't been born. I was looking for deals, special deals! Had it been someone else, heh-heh-heh! But with me, it all came to nothing. Everything goes downhill with me. Only misfortune comes my way! It hurts to talk about it. Cut your nose to spite your face . . . it's no more than nothing."

It was very clear that things were not going smoothly with my Reb Alter. He had troubles. But as long as his tongue had loosened, a wee little push was all that was needed to keep it wagging. I was of no mind to prevent this. I gave him a good push, and my Alter was on the move, telling about his misfortune in his unique way:

"Anyway, I go to the fair in Yarmelinetz. When I arrive at the market place, I unhitch the wagon in the square, you understand, and unpack my bit of goods. Well, to make a long story short—nothing! I stand there waiting for customers. What brought me to this fair, God only

34

knows. I, it shouldn't happen to you, am in a tight spot right now. The printer wants his money. Well, that's a small matter—so he wants it. But he wants, you understand, to stop giving me goods! My older daughter is not getting any younger. A girl of her age, you understand, should be getting married. So I have to find her a husband. There are plenty of bachelors, but a husband, you understand, a husband is not so easy to find! And then, with all this going on, my wife decides to have a baby boy, and when? Just before Passover! You understand me? A boy! You know what that means? But—nothing!"

"Don't be offended with me," I said to Alter, "for interrupting you. But why, at your age, did you marry a young wife who has children so easily?"

"God protect you!" cried Alter in amazement. "I had to have a housewife to take care of the household. What does a Jew want to get married for at all? All the poor man wants is a good housewife."

"Tell me then, Reb Alter," I asked, "why did you divorce your first wife and ruin her whole life? She was a good housewife."

"*Beh!*" Alter winced, looking wretched.

"Nor was she a sterile woman, glory to His Holy Name, this first wife of yours," I persisted in the same vein. "What happened to your poor children by your first marriage? Do you know?"

"*Beh!*" Alter scratched under his prayer curl uncomfortably, waved his hand helplessly and sighed from the depths of his heart.

"*Beh*" is a priceless word for us Jews. It has so many meanings and serves to answer so many difficult questions. "*Beh*" can be used at any time during a conversation and will always be in place. A Jew in a difficult situation, with

35

his back to the wall, can always wriggle out of it with one word: *"Beh!"* A swindler or a bankrupt will use *"beh"* as a payment to his creditors when they press him too hard. *"Beh"* stands by a man in time of need, as, for example, when the poor fellow is caught telling a lie. *"Beh"* is a fitting comment to one who has been drumming in your ears for hours on end and you haven't listened to or heard a word of what he said. *"Beh"* is the apology of a bigwig who has hoodwinked the public; of a man of reputed virtue whose true character has finally been uncovered. In a word, *"beh"* has a variety of tastes and all sorts of interpretations, such as, for example: come, if you dare! the goose is cooked! I'm on your side! do your worst! a plague upon you! A Jewish mind will always divine the proper meaning of *"beh"* under the given circumstances. The direction in which the barb is aimed will always be clear.

Alter's last *"beh"* was a bitter one. Contrition, repentance and self-accusation seemed to be wrapped up in it. Surely, his mean treatment of his first wife and their children must have left a wound in his heart. He must have seen in the many misfortunes that had befallen him a punishment for his sins. This was clearly expressed by the bitter heartfelt sigh, by the helpless way he waved his hand, and also by the sheepish scratching under his prayer curl, as if to say: "Bite your lip and keep your mouth shut! The devil take you!"

I was angry with myself for having scratched Alter's old wounds. That is the trouble with a Jew who must needs butt into someone's personal affairs and get under his skin with all sorts of questions, while all the time the poor man is choking down his troubles in silence. In addition, I was angry with myself because I would have to

36

start all over again. After loosening Alter's tongue so that it was merrily wagging away like clockwork, I had to touch a little wheel and make the pendulum grind to a halt! I fell back on my former tactic. Once more I fed him hints about the possibility of our trading. I was not stingy; I gave him a full measure of the tongue loosener. I found the little key that fitted him, wound him up so gently that he did not even notice, and soon the pendulum was swinging merrily again.

of it. To make a long story short, I cracked the whip and things started moving. I ran from Reb Elyokum to Reb Getzl and from Reb Getzl to Reb Elyokum. I was now running around, blessed be His Name, like the best of them. I sweated and strained. The match had to go through, and right here, at the fair. Why not? Is there a better place than a fair?

"To cut it short, the two merchants were in a big hurry: they looked each other over in passing, liked each other, wanted each other—wanted each other badly! *Nu,* who could ask for anything better? The two of them were straining at the leash. . . . I tell you, I could have hugged myself! My commission was as good as in my pocket. I had decided how much dowry to settle on my daughter. I was already bargaining with a ragpicker for an old satin coat for myself. Shirts were my last worry. They could wait until later. The good Lord would provide . . . Well, to make a long story short—nothing! Just listen to what had to happen to me! I tell you, a man with no luck is better off not being born. Just as we were ready to break the pots in celebration, we happened to remember the bride and groom, and what do you think? Believe me, it hurts to even talk about it. The whole thing was a flop! No, it was ten times worse than a flop! It just blew up in my face! Listen to my misfortune and how the wrath of God descended on me: the two merchants each had—what do you think they had? They each had a son!"

"What do you mean, Reb Alter?" I shot out in a peal of laughter. "How can that be? You would never do anything as foolish as that! How could you arrange a match before finding out which of the two parties has a son and which a daughter?"

"Of course, it's simple enough!" Alter winced in vexa-

40

tion. "I still have as much sense as anyone else and nobody has to teach me how to live! Who ever heard of a Jew who doesn't know how matches are made? Reb Mendele, you know what our customs concerning matchmaking and marriages are like. Then why are you so surprised at my misfortune? It could have happened to anybody.

"I knew that Reb Elyokum was supposed to have a marriageable daughter—and what a daughter! May I have such a jewel myself! I saw her last year with my own eyes, may I see Paradise just as surely! But when a man has no luck, everything he knows is worth nothing! How was I supposed to know that this beautiful girl was in a hurry, that she had rushed off, and got herself married? She must have been seized by some fever. I didn't know a thing about it, may I know as much about my poverty! Now, let me ask you, whom could I have meant when I started working on this match between Reb Elyokum and Reb Getzl? Reb Elyokum's daughter, of course! His daughter and Reb Getzl's son! It was so clear that people would have laughed at me if I'd said anything about it. Everybody knows that two males don't get married! A male marries a female—that's our custom! How else could it be? All I know is that I did what was right. No one else, as I am a Jew, could have done any better.

"To make a long story short, I had worked fast: the important things—the dowry and living quarters for the couple—were all settled. Don't forget, at a fair with two busy merchants, there's no time for empty talk or nonsense. Each word counts. You have to come right to the point without wasting time. That's my story. Now, let's take Reb Elyokum. When I first brought up the match, he must have been sure that the talk was about his son. How else? He himself wasn't going to marry Reb Getzl! And he'd never imagine that his daughter was meant when he knew very well that he had a son and not a daughter to marry off. So that's his story and you can see that both sides are right. But nothing. Now, do you understand?"

"*Beh!*" I said, barely able to contain my laughter and straining to keep a straight face.

"*Nu,* thank God for making you understand!" Alter pointed his thumb at me and, with raised eyebrows, drawled a knowing "Aha!" as if my "*Beh!*" had hit the nail on the head.

To tell the truth, Alter's explanation did make a certain amount of sense. Why not? Considering the way we Jews arrange our matches, why shouldn't such a thing occur? Unconsciously, I again said, "*Beh!*" and looked at Alter in a most friendly way.

"Aha!" said Alter, pointing his thumb at me again. "Aha, so now you understand! But nothing . . . I'm not finished yet. I still had hopes about patching things up. Once I start something, I don't give up so easily, if you know what I mean."

"Reb Alter, God have mercy on you! What are you talking about?" I actually jumped up in amazement, feeling certain that the terrible heat had made Alter lose his mind. "What kind of hope could you have had when both fathers had only sons?"

"Don't get excited," Alter soothed me. "It wasn't as bad as that, Reb Mendele. I had another idea. When God visits a plague on us, He also provides the remedy. You see, I still had Reb Berl Teletza to fall back on. He had plenty of eligible daughters. As a matter of fact, right from the start, those three names danced around in my head—Elyokum, Getzl, Teletza. It was just my luck to pick the wrong pair and leave Teletza out. The best way to patch things up was to bring Teletza into the picture, the honorable Reb Berishl! To make a long story short, I tried to smooth over my blunder with both merchants. Wasn't it everybody's fault—mine a little, theirs a little, and also our luck a little? It was probably not ordained by heaven, not in the cards, you understand? Then I started on the list of praises for Reb Berishl: he was, may the Evil Eye not harm him, wealthy, good-natured, generous to charities, an honored member in many societies. After all, this was Reb Berishl, no less! I didn't have to say anything about what a sage he was: you never have to say anything about a rich man's wisdom—it's understood. But, nothing! My hopes rose like dough with yeast. 'It will all turn out for the best yet,' I said to myself. 'Elyokum's and Getzl's sons have to get married and Teletza's daughters are like made to order! God willing, Reb Berishl is the answer to all my troubles.'

"To make a long story short, I had the runs again— back and forth at full steam. The arrangements were going along well enough. Things were looking up. But, nothing! Suddenly, the fair was over. The stores closed, the wagons drove off, the people disappeared, and I was left alone in the empty market square! All my hard work, all my aggravation, was thrown out!

"Now, do you understand?" Alter appealed to me in a plaintive beseeching voice, stretching out both hands. "Do you see what I mean? When you have no luck, then all the wisdom in the world won't help! *Oy*, the wrath of God has been upon me for a long time. It's a punishment for my sins. And you talk to me about doing business on a cash basis? I don't even have a groshen to my name, woe is me!"

"Ai, just like in the bathhouse!" I said, and moved away.

Alter glared at me with eyes wide open, shaking his head. Highly incensed, he turned and spoke, as though to the world at large:

"What a crooked, false-hearted man! Oh, enemies of Zion, here I am in agony, my troubles are breaking my heart, and he? Nothing! He's just thinking about himself, that's all! I can see right through the whole act! I know the Jewish tricks. I can tell pretty well when a man wants to back out of an offer as soon as he finds out that he doesn't have a cash customer! I can tell when a man doesn't want to do business."

"Really . . ." I exclaimed and tugged at Alter's beard playfully. "How can such thoughts even occur to you, Reb Alter? I meant something entirely different. The way your story ended with the disbanding of the fair reminded me of a very interesting tale which I can't forget to this very day. It's a story about a bathhouse and it ends just like yours. There's not even a hair's breadth difference between them, except the other story is short. It's worth hearing. Oho, you're sweating, Reb Alter. Move over a little, if you please, and we'll be able to lie here with our backs to the sun and talk."

Alter wiped the perspiration from his face with the back of his sleeve. From his bosom pocket, he brought out a meerschaum pipe with a female figure painted on the bowl. He cleaned the mouthpiece and the beaded stem with a short piece of wire which hung from a chain attached to the bowl cover. He lit the pipe, took a peek at the female figure and settled back in all his glory under the tree. I cleared my throat and began my tale.

V

"FOR A LONG TIME, A YOUNG FELLOW LIVED IN THE STONE bathhouse of Glupsk; his name was Fishke the Lame. Neither I nor anyone else ever thought of inquiring just who Fishke was and where he came from. It didn't matter! Somehow or other a creature, a Fishke, existed in our midst—a creature like so many other wretched souls who appear among us children of Israel, from nowhere, like toadstools after a rainstorm, full-blown, with all their earmarks, without giving the slightest hint that they are budding and about to burst into bloom! Paupers live in their obscure holes and make children quietly. Who cares? They are fruitful and multiply on the face of the earth. The harvest, may the Evil Eye not harm them, is great. And then the young ones suddenly stand on their own feet and a fresh crop of new, quivering little Jews makes its appearance in the world: little Fishkes, little Chaikes, Chaims, Yosels—naked, barefoot, clad in rags, cluttering up the houses, the synagogues, the streets, the towns, and getting between everyone's feet.

"It would be hard to call Fishke handsome. He had a big flat head and a large broad mouth with yellow crooked teeth. He lisped, could not pronounce an "r" and limped badly. Fishke was getting on in years. As far as he was concerned, he could have been married for a long time and would have gladly blessed Glupsk with his share of children. But as his foul luck would have it, he had been by-passed and, as we say in our book-peddling business, had become a 'shelf item.' He had even been forgotten during the recruiting of 'cholera grooms,' that is, when the *Kahal* of Glupsk snatched the most hideous cripples, beggars and vagrants and frantically married them off to each other in the cemetery among the tombstones in order to frighten the epidemic away.

"The first time this happened, *Kahal* chose to honor not Fishke but the famous cripple Yontl who had no legs and moved around on his seat by pushing himself with two little wooden blocks. He was mated with a well-known beggar woman who had teeth like spades and no underlip. The cholera epidemic was so terror-stricken by this pair that it wiped out a good part of the population in its fright, after which it took to its heels and fled.

"The second time, Fishke was again by-passed in favor of Nechemtsieh the Village Idiot. Before an assemblage of city notables, all of them fine Jews, at the cemetery, this poor fool placed the bridal crown and cover on the head of a girl whose head had been covered since childhood because of its cankerous sores and about whom it was rumored that she was, pardon the expression, a hermaphrodite. It was said that the assembled crowd made unusually merry at this wedding and that an ocean of brandy was consumed among the tombstones. 'That's fine,' was the general comment. 'Let them multiply, let the children of Israel replenish the earth in the face of the cholera. Let the poor cripples enjoy themselves also . . .' But that's not my point.

"To make a long story short, *Kahal* had forgotten Fishke. Once again the cholera came to Glupsk and still it did not help Fishke. He remained a bachelor as before. Even Auntie Noseless, whose partner scraped away on a sort of a fiddle while she did a jig in the middle of the

46

street and accompanied him in a thin falsetto, even Auntie had forgotten about Fishke—Auntie, who collected alms in a little plate so that the corpses might dance, so that cripples and beggars should have a few groschen with which to get married. Even good-hearted Auntie let Fishke go on without a wife. It certainly was a pity, but such was his luck.

"Fishke usually walked around barefoot, with no coat, in a coarse patched shirt with long greasy tails and pants of coarse linen which hung in many folds. His job was to walk through the streets and cry, 'Gentlemen, to the steam bath!' on Fridays, and 'Little ladies, to the steam bath!' on Wednesdays. In the summertime, when garden produce became available his eel-like voice could be heard throughout the Jewish quarter: 'Everybody here! Young garlic, everybody!' In the bathhouse, he watched the clothes; or he fetched someone a kettle of water with his dirty shirt sleeve plugged into the spout; or, tossing it from hand to hand with great skill, a red-hot coal with which to light someone's cigar. For this, he might sometimes be thrown two or three kopecks. Because of his job at the bathhouse he was allowed certain privileges which were granted to religious officials, such as: going from house to house with the band of bathhouse employees on *Chanukah* and *Purim* to receive the customary few kopecks; to be invited to the circumcision of a rich man's son where he could drink a toast and eat some honey cake; to go to the rich peoples' houses with a basket during Passover and be given the broken pieces of *matzo*.

"I knew Fishke very well. I used to enjoy getting him into a conversation and listening to his colorful expressions. He was by no means as foolish as he looked. When-

47

ever I come to Glupsk, the first thing I do is to go to the stone bathhouse, have the lice removed from my clothes and stockings, and steam my body through to the bone on the topmost bench. Say what you will, but this is my greatest delight. What can be better than being steamed through and perspiring? I tell you once more, I would even enjoy perspiring right now, if the sun weren't shining into my eyes.

"Move over a bit, Reb Alter! Oho! You're not perspiring so badly yourself, may the Evil Eye not harm you! Move over a little, please, that's the way."

"*Nu*, let's get to the point!" Alter grumbled irritably. "I think you have enough room now. And please, don't drag it out so much. Cut it short."

"Be patient, Reb Alter! The day is still young," I said and continued my narration.

"Several years ago I happened to be in Glupsk walking along a street when I saw Fishke from afar. I almost jumped with surprise. There, indeed, was my old Fishke with his lame legs, but dressed like a dandy in a brand-new Circassian overcoat and new shoes and stockings. On his head he wore a big fur cap and under his coat was a new shirt, starched hard as a board, and embroidered with red flowers. What did this mean, I wondered. Could it be that *Kahal* had picked him as a cholera groom after all? But there had been no cholera epidemic in Glupsk that year—not because the polluted lake nearby had been drained, or because the piles of stinking mud and the dead cats had been removed from the streets, or because the homeowners had decided to fly in the face of tradition and stop emptying their garbage pails in front of their houses under the noses of passers-by. No, no, God forbid! How could one ever accuse a Jewish community of such action!

49

"For the benefit of the men of good birth, the bath was kept well heated. The big and the small, the old and the young, were whipping and washing themselves with gusto. The crowd groaned and sighed, smacked its lips with pleasure. At that point, I climbed up to the uppermost benches and, lying down in a corner so as to be alone, began to steam my aching bones and body.

"*Oy*, Reb Alter! Move over a bit. A little more into the shade, if you please."

Alter looked at me as at some scourge from the devil and shrugged his shoulders, "*Nu, nu!*"

"Take your time," I soothed him. "Why the rush? Soon, soon. But let me catch my breath first."

VI

ALTER FUSSED FOR A WHILE WITH THE MOUTHPIECE OF HIS pipe. It was badly clogged. He finally twisted it out of the bowl, cursing in anger, and set a goose quill in its place. He lit it again—puff, puff, puff—and a dense cloud of smoke poured out like from a chimney. I straightened my old bones a bit and continued my tale.

"I arrived at the bathhouse early the next morning, long before the crowd collected. Berl the Whipper sat on a bench between two stacks of reeds which stood on end like towers. He inspected them earnestly, like a woman picking peas, and bound them into brooms. Nearby, at the stove, stood Itzik the Watchman, a man with a broad beard who had been earning his living for thirty years by doing nothing more than keeping his eye on the bundles of clothing with his hands folded over his stomach, and wishing the wealthy gentlemen a "May you prosper" as they left the bathhouse. He stretched his arms up high and yawned out loud. He figured up how much money his wife would want for *Shabbes,* and discussed with Berl the meager earnings they received, imitated each of the rich men individually and complained that the customers were not what they used to be. In the good old days, even the most godforsaken miser left no less than six kopecks, and today . . . He spat: 'Today, may they all go to the devil!'

"Berl and Itzik gave me a warm welcome. It was a long time since I had been there last and they considered me to be an honored guest. We talked about many things. Fi-

Why then should her grandchild blacken her face in her old age and ruin the family name? No, sir! He refused to have anything to do with this match or the bride, even if she were covered with gold."

" ' " 'If you don't like it, you can lump it!' he said. 'As far as I'm concerned the comedy is over.'

" ' "We stood there open-mouthed. Actually, we don't care so much about losing the groom as about losing the dinner. What are we going to do with this feast, with such fish and such roasts? We've run ourselves ragged all day getting everything ready. We didn't even get our commission for arranging the match. It's a sin to let all this work go to waste, our effort, our hard work! We thought and thought and finally we got an idea—Fishke! Let him help us out of our trouble! Let him be the groom. What's the difference? Why should he care? And that's why we're here—to lead him to the *chupeh* instead of the porter!"

" 'Just as they finished their story, Fishke arrived. Oh, we weren't going to let a bargain like this slip through our fingers. We didn't bother him with long explanations. We just shoved him along: "Go, young man, with your crooked legs. Under the *chupeh* with you! You've been single long enough."

" 'It was all done very quickly. Before Fishke had time to look around, the fish and the roasts were gobbled up, the wine and the brandy had disappeared, and everybody was congratulating the newlyweds.

" 'That's why Fishke is strolling around in a brand new Circassian overcoat, meant for the porter, looking like a dandy. Every morning he leads his blind wife to her place at the cemetery and every evening he brings her home. Food and drink are no longer a worry for Fishke. His wife wears the pants. She has a good trade and brings home a steady income. They both love each other, and would be hard put to find, God forbid, fault with each other.' "

"And this, Reb Alter, was what Berl the Whipper told me. Now do you see," I exclaimed, "what miracles can happen in the world?

"Do you see how among us Jews the lame and the blind are paired? How our weddings are arranged? How the fate of couples is decided, and for what purpose? So that the marriage brokers may eat and drink till they burst! That is how it is among the poor and also among the rich, except that when the rich marry, it's a different type of dinner with a different taste. . . . But that's not my point.

"Don't worry, Reb Alter! If you haven't yet succeeded in making a match between two men then you will surely succeed, with God's help, in making some other kind of match. Don't give up! You started your matchmaking like an experienced broker. Just because the young fellow . . . well, *beh!* Upon my word! But once you come across an eligible young lady, things will be different! Whether she's blind, deaf, dumb—'Go, daughter o'mine! Under the *chupeh* with you and my best wishes! The printer needs money. My mare has to eat. My daughter must get married. My wife has just borne me a son, God praise him. Go then, daughter o'mine! Under the *chupeh* with you?'

"Reb Alter! Move over a little more, please. Oho, how you're sweating, may the Evil Eye not harm you! You're as wet as a beaver!"

VII

"WELL, I FEEL LOW IN ANY CASE," ALTER MUTTERED TO himself with a groan. He looked sad and big beads of sweat stood out on his forehead. He raised his eyes and looked at me imploringly—just as an infant looks at its mother when it wants the breast. But poor Alter only meant business with his glance. He yearned to do a little trading with me. After all, how can two Jews with fully grown beards simply lie under a tree at the height of day and do nothing? If two Jews happened to be marooned on a desert island in the middle of the ocean, just the two of them without another living soul, then it is quite certain that with the passing of time one of them would open some sort of little store and the other one—also a little business. They would trade with each other. One would borrow from the other at a certain rate of interest and thus they would both manage to earn their keep.

Alter soon teased, "What does my lordship have in his wagon today?" But to me it sounded like, "Mommy, more . . ."

"Unpack your goods, Reb Mendl, and let's see what you have."

Since I had no choice, there was no point in being lazy. I unpacked my wares, and Alter his. Before long, we were absorbed in a heated session of estimating, bargaining, making exchanges. I tried to sell him some books with uneven print and missing lines: I had been wanting to

58

get rid of them for a long time. But he was no fool and wouldn't even touch them.

"That stuff will never move," Alter said, wrinkling his nose. "It's just trash written by some shabby bench warmers! God knows what they have scribbled there. Who wants it? Nobody can understand a word of it. It must be written in Turkish! Books like that are only dust collectors. It's a waste of space to take them along. *Feh!* Show me something interesting, Reb Mcndele!"

I brought out my collection of weekday prayer books, festival prayer books, prayer books for women, *Haggadas* —one sort after another. But my Alter was squeamish and found fault with each one. One book did captivate him, though. He looked at it and couldn't tear himself away. It was really quite an antique. The pages were all of different colors and also different sizes. The letters were smudged and unclear and of different types: Rashi type, diamond, pearl, extended and bold-face types. The composition of each page was a marvel to behold. It was laid out in strips—narrow ones with small print on both sides, a broad strip with bigger type in the center, and below this, a belly of tiny type set in like poppy seeds; and, between these patches of print, stretched narrow ribbons of blank space across the page and up and down, like little pathways in the forest. These are some of the qualities that a Jew in our part of the world looks for in a book.

Of course, the pages did not follow in sequence either. In this lay the whole genius of the arrangement: a Jew ought to break his head a bit and figure out the proper sequence. There is no point in dwelling on typographical errors. It stands to reason that there were myriads of them. And who cared? A Jew has a good mind and it wouldn't hurt him to use it to figure out what was meant. But the style made up for all the other faults. The style was delightfully intricate, simply impossible to understand. Just the thing to satisfy the most demanding Jewish taste. Because, when all is said and done, what we Jews appreciate most is something we must break our teeth on and still be unsuccessful in getting it. After all, if you can't understand it, there must be something to it. . . . But that's not my point.

My Alter seized this merchandise with both hands. His health seemed to improve visibly just from handling it. Then we started trading:

women's books of supplication for the *Tales of Baba;*
women's homilies for *A Thousand and One Nights;*
prayer scrolls for good luck charms;
penitential prayers from Zhitomir for prayer shawls from
　　Berszed;
lamentations from Vilna for rams'-horns;
Chanukah candles for wolves'-teeth talismans;
brass Sabbath candlesticks for children's shiny skullcaps.

Although not a single kopeck passed through our hands, we were both immensely pleased with the trading process itself. After all, we had both been swapping, bartering, trafficking, giving and taking, and keeping very busy.

Alter's melancholy had blown away like smoke. A glance at his face made it clear that his humiliating experiences with the matchmaking at the fair in Yarmelinez were now completely forgotten. Quietly he did some calculations on his fingers. His head was cocked to one side, as though some inner bookkeeper sat in it to whose figures Alter paid rapt attention. It seemed that the tally indicated some future profit, with God's help, because his mouth spread from ear to ear under his bushy mustache, and his whole face broke out in a bright smile.

In the meanwhile, evening drew near and it was time to say our prayers. A caressing breeze blew up, and tatters of clouds, which we had awaited like long overdue guests, appeared in the sky. The trees began to rock slowly. They bent their heads toward one another and carried on a whispered conversation after having been silent all day. The breeze awakened the sleeping grain. The stalks woke up noisily like young children and kissed each other again and again. God's creatures were in motion all over: in the fields, in the forest and in the air. One after another the little songbirds stepped forth on the branches of the trees and saplings. They preened their little feathers, wiped their little beaks, cocked their little heads and broke out in sweet song. Butterflies, richly clad in satins and silks, in antique style with precious jewels, danced and whirled in the air; they soared, turned, swooped down and showed off their charms.

Two storks, like guardsmen with long red legs, stood on the grass with beaks raised in the air and glared about in proud defiance. A mischievous little bird flitted from tree to tree calling, "Cuckoo, cuckoo!" as though it were playing hide-and-seek. From the stalks of corn and wheat came an answering call: "Pick-ber-wick! Pick-ber-wick!" as if to say, "You'll never catch me. Pour salt on my tail and see how much good that does. You'll never, never catch me."

In a nearby thicket, the nightingale trilled. Up and down the scale he went, thrilling the soul, putting all the world-famous cantors to shame. Even the frogs in the marshes did their share and croaked hoarsely. Nor were the flies and bees quiet; and the crickets, little thieves,

61

chirped everywhere. For this kind of concert a ticket at any price was cheap. . . . The whole world had come alive and was full of joy. What a pleasure to hear, see and smell the sounds, the sights, the odors all around!

"Reb Alter, it's good! Reb Alter, it's beautiful! It makes your heart leap with joy. God's world is alive! God's world is wonderful! Oh, how I'd like to plunge in, head first . . ."

"Reb Mendele, shame on you!" Reb Alter admonished me. "It's time for our evening prayers. And you'd better remember to start right at the beginning and not let your mind wander."

I pulled up my stockings, tightened my belt and began to recite my prayers lustily in a high-pitched voice. My Alter, may he live long, followed suit and accompanied me in his thick-stringed bass. Thus we both sang our praises to His dear Name, while all the bushes and flowers in the fields and all the birds and beasts in the woods burst into song and gave their thanks to God.

Reb Alter ran through his prayers in a hurry. While I was still only halfway through, he produced a small keg of grease from somewhere under his wagon and busily began to smear his wheels with it.

"Don't dally, Reb Mendele. Hurry it up a bit," he drove me. "Get your wagon ready while I go after the horses. It's time to leave. We can travel a good ways before night falls."

Alter left and I began to do justice to my wagon. I didn't hurry. I smeared the wheels leisurely, without sparing the grease and inspected each axle individually and in detail. This took a while. When I had finished, my Alter had still not returned. The horses must have strayed far into the woods to eat their fill. The sun sank below the horizon. The last rays climbed down the trees on which they had played with such joy and brilliance only a short while ago and said, "Good night!" to the forest. . . .

And then I was struck by fear. Maybe Alter had fallen ill? This was no laughing matter after sweating so heavily and fasting all day! Maybe he was lying somewhere in a faint! Or maybe someone had attacked him? After all, it was a forest, an out-of-the-way place! I couldn't sit here doing nothing, I had to go and see. I took heart and entered the forest. I walked and searched but in vain. Alter and the horses had vanished into thin air. I walked further until I came to a long narrow valley which seemed to divide the forest in two. This valley was overgrown with brambles and small thorny bushes. On the one side it led toward the highway and on the other side to God alone knows where. The forest stood in silent slumber, covered from above with a dark quilt. It was quiet all around. Only on occasion, two tall trees, close neighbors, whispered to each other with heads bent close, tickling each other from behind with their branches. Or a few leaves flapped, moved as though they were upset and could not rest. This was the forest talking in its sleep. It was dreaming of the day that had just ended, with all its joys and sorrows. The murmur of the reeds—that was the forest dreaming of the poor trees which had been chopped down before their time. The noise of something falling —that was a dream of a nest of innocent little birds which the murderous hawk had destroyed, and this was also why the leaves were restless. They were flapping over the dead mother and her murdered young. A cloud of melancholy descended upon the forest and enveloped me too.

Fantasy, that terrible prankster and notorious liar, began to play havoc with my thoughts. He shipped me a

63

supply of wild and terrifying images and my mental factory reworked this raw material and made it even more fantastic. In this shipment I found a corpse, the murdered Alter Yaknehoz, and the bones of our horses. My mind refined upon this and developed it into a fiery red monster and a wolf of tremendous size with huge frightening teeth. . . .

I was about to descend into the valley when the thought occurred to me that I had left the two wagons standing unattended in the middle of the field. Neither sight nor smell of our small fortunes would remain. It would be wisest to go back and check before doing anything else. It was also possible that Alter had returned with the horses long ago and was now beginning to worry about me. This thought settled in my mind and gave me renewed strength. My hopes grew and grew until they tore to shreds the clouds of melancholy and allowed a few rays of peace to shine upon my troubled heart.

I hastened back to the wagons.

VIII

WITH GOD'S HELP I ARRIVED IN ONE PIECE WITHOUT BROKEN
limbs although, in my haste, I had walked into a tree more
than once. Rising from a fall in the forest is by no means
as embarrassing as in town where people gather around
and laugh. Therefore, each time I raised myself from the
ground, I did it with pleasure and thanked the Lord for
being able to do so with dignity. And since God, in His
mercy, was so generous to me, I felt I had reason to believe that when I arrived I would find my Alter and the
horses. But I had not deserved that much charity from
His beloved Name.

Alter was not there.

I was petrified. God alone knew what had happened
to Alter and where his remains lay now. This time his
dismal luck had really shown what it could do. And what
was I to do? What would happen to me? That was a problem. My plan had been to unload my wares in Glupsk,
stock up there with as many copies of the *Book of Lamentations* as possible and distribute them in surrounding
towns and villages, as I did every year at this time. The
"Three Weeks" were almost upon us. I couldn't afford
to lose an hour. If I lost time on the road, the Jews in the
towns and villages would be without their *Books of Lamentations*. This was no laughing matter—Jews without
Books of Lamentations!

I could just imagine what would happen on *Tisha
B'ov:* Jews would gobble up their *milchikeh* noodles, fill

their bellies with hard-boiled eggs dipped in ash, and would seat themselves sullenly on the ground in their stocking feet showing their worn-out heels. The young mischief-makers would be ready to throw their stockpiles of burrs at a moment's notice. Everyone would wait for the beginning, for the good word, and suddenly—no *Books of Lamentations!* The black plague must have taken Mendele, he didn't bring the *Lamentations!* Ten men to one Book. What shoving and crowding! What a confusion of lice! What a tangling of beards! And side curls full of burrs! And the stench of eggs and noodles rising into everyone's nostrils. . . . The women would not be nearly as badly off. To them it mattered little whether it was the *Lamentations.* Anything would do so long as it was in print: *Techinas, Festival prayer books, Haggadahs*—it was all the same! They'd wail over them in their high-pitched voices. What difference did it make, if only they could have a good cry? Yes, it was a nasty situation any way you looked at it . . . but that's beside the point.

I had to do something. I could not just sit idly by with folded hands. The search had to continue. I looked at the stars and remembered that it was time to eat. Out came my little satchel. I took a few gulps from the bottle, bul-bul-bul, to ease my troubles, snatched a few bites to eat, only for appearance's sake, bid farewell to the bottle, bul-bul-bul again, and set off in haste.

Once again I was in the forest, once again near the valley, and soon in the valley itself. But to tell the truth, I was not alone, nor was my heart as heavy as before. Yes, this time I had company. We talked about my troubles and I was cheered.

When I took my hurried snack after fasting all day, I

must have spent too much time with the bottle. An extra sip on an empty stomach and I was over the limit. Besides, I had hardly eaten anything. With all the excitement and fright, I had lost my appetite. I couldn't force anything down my throat. Well, this extra sip stood by me in this time of need like a father. It gave me courage and made me very talkative, may I be protected from this today. I've always been that way—an extra lick of brandy on Purim or *Simches-Torah* and the words began to flow like from a sack full of holes. I could talk to a wall and smile ever so sweetly. I became so good and soft—you could use me for a compress on a boil. My body stretched and became light, and thin as weak tea. Jumbled little pieces of Mendele bounced around—hard to tell which was the most important one. At that point, it used to seem as though I turned into two Mendeles, one pulling east and the other west. The pair of feet that they shared tripped over each other not knowing which one to follow. One Mendele asks, the other one answers. My words came back at me from afar, like an echo, not like my voice at all. The tone had the ring of an empty barrel. Nevertheless, I did not lose my head completely. A trace of sense remained, as in a dream.

"Good evening!" I bowed. "And where are you off to this time of night?"

"*Ta* . . . addle-heads, asses!" answered the other Mendele with a good-natured little smile. "They decided to get lost. A farce, upon my word!"

"There's a hole there, Reb Mendele. Take care!"

"Yes, as I am Jew, there's a hole! This must be at least the twentieth time I've fallen, I'm sure!"

"Get up then, if you please. It's not respectable to lie there stretched out like that."

"Thanks for the advice, uncle! Well, I'm up again. I'll try feeling my way with the whip. It's a comedy, upon my word! The trees are walking! Here's to your health, let's walk together! *Feh*, don't scratch like that! *Ai*, another scratch! Almost took my eye out that time, *tfu!*"

"Spit on them, Reb Mendele! It's the only way to get rid of them. Here, follow this little path, if you please, and you'll come out in the open field."

"Good, I'm here already. Oh, what a moon! Like a hunk of dough! A real moon, like in Odessa, with a nose and eyes. *Sha,* should I say the prayer to the moon? Peace unto you!

"And unto you, peace!"

"Peace unto you!"

"And unto you, peace! Just as I spring toward you and cannot reach you. . . . Then jump, uncle!"

"Hup, hup, hup! Just so shall my enemies be unable to reach me. . . . What is it that they want from us anyway?" I sobbed suddenly. "Is it my fault that I'm alive and must eat? Here, look at my body! You call that a body? It's as thin as a rail! Always sick! Always in pain. I had a mother once, she petted me and kissed me. Woe is me, I'm an orphan, an orphan!" I wept in earnest.

"Sha, sha!" came the encouraging reply. "You know it can't be helped. How is it that an elderly Jew with a beard, with a wife and horde of children, isn't ashamed to weep out in the open with the moon watching! It just shows a lack of respect! Stop crying, the devil won't take you. Better keep your eyes open, here's a fence."

"Yes, as I am a Jew, a fence indeed. I've walked right into it, as a matter of fact. What shall I do now?"

"Why, just climb over it. That's the way."

"Thanks for the advice, uncle. Now I've got both my feet in the garden."

"Well, congratulations, cousin! Now, march on, if you please."

"Be calm. I'm going. My, what a crop! Chick-peas, beans, and cucumbers without end!"

"Bless the fruits of the earth, then, and don't wait for a second invitation."

"What delicious cucumbers! May they multiply! Hah, what hit me? Who's that?"

The blows came from a sturdy peasant who had come up behind me and was letting me know that it's impolite to prowl around in other people's gardens. The point he was getting at was that it is wrong to steal fresh cucumbers at night. The blows on the one hand and the fresh cucumbers on the other made me sober up. For a moment I stood befuddled, as though I had just awakened from sleep. Naturally, the first words out of my mouth were, *"G'vald!"* Help! But I reconsidered this approach and decided to act unconcerned. I turned to the peasant and asked him winningly, in coarse Ukrainian: "You didn't happen to see a little Jew with a couple of horses passing by here by any chance, did you?"

But the peasant's mind was made up. He wouldn't be swayed, nor would he listen. He pulled me along by the sleeve, he shoved me from behind and just kept on repeating, "Move along! Move along!" It was no use. I stumbled along until at last we arrived at a house with lit-up windows. In front of it stood a *britchka* harnessed with four good horses.

On entering the house, the peasant shoved me ahead while he doffed his cap and took up a position near the

69

door. Not knowing what else to do, I took my cap off also. I scratched my head and felt terribly out of place.

At a desk sat a little clerk busily scribbling with a scraping pen which begged for ink every few minutes. No sooner was its mouth filled than it would spit it all out on the paper. The little clerk was impatient with the pen. He winced and cursed at every dip. It was obvious that this was torture for both of them, poor things. They were both unhappy: the pen with his heavy hand and shameful mistakes; he with the maddening blots. He—a squeeze; the pen—a blot. In the middle of the room stood a red collar with brass buttons, a big belly, and a puffy, glistening face, with small bloodshot eyes. This creature twisted his mustaches. His voice, booming out of his double chin, spoke harshly to two men with hanging heads who stood to a side of the door. The first one was tall, with a powerful body, a shaven neck and a silver earring in his left earlobe. The other one was thin with a pointed little beard, a tin badge on his chest, and a long stick which he held with both hands, squinting continually and bowing every few minutes. The red collar was furious. He roared at the first one: "Some village elder you are! To Siberia in chains with you!" And to the second one: "I'll slice you into thin strips, you sot! You so-and-so, the devil take your mother!"

Each of my limbs died separately. I shook as though in high fever. There was a buzzing in my head and a ringing in my ears. I couldn't hear, I couldn't see what was happening. I did not even hear properly what charges the peasant made against me. But when the red collar hiccoughed and turned to me with his harsh Russian speech, I suddenly woke up and heard everything. Before my eyes a fist waved and terrible words assaulted my ears:

70

"Thief, contraband, smuggler, pickpocket, chains, prison, the knout, Siberia . . ." Suddenly he seized one of my prayer curls and, angrily imitating my grimace of pain, he snatched a scissors from the desk and, in a rage, snipped off the entire curl!

Seeing my prayer curl on the floor, I burst into tears—my old, gray prayer curl which had been with me from childhood until now; my prayer curl which had shared the joys and pains of an entire lifetime! Why, my mother had fondled it, combed it, and took pride in its shiny black waves when I was a boy. It was an adornment on my face in days gone by, when I was young and fresh. The poor thing became prematurely gray from troubles and worry, and I was not, God forfend, one bit ashamed of its grayness. We had both aged early from poverty, loneliness, afflictions, threats, uncalled-for enmity and persecution from the rest of the world. Oh whom, good Lord, had it offended? Whom, I ask, had my gray hairs harmed?

My heart wept within me, "G'vald," silently. I stared mutely like a lamb at shearing time and from my eyes—drip, drip, drip, big tears like chick-peas . . . My cheek smarted in its newly acquired nakedness. My appearance must have changed terribly. It must have been a pitiful sight indeed, because the red collar lost his power of speech and softened, putting his hands on both my shoulders. It seems that a human heart beat under those brass buttons. My gray hairs and my whole appearance convinced him of my honesty. As if in apology to me, he fell angrily upon the peasant, demanding why, for a cucumber, he dragged a poor old man around. With a hiccough, he drove the peasant out. Then, taking his cap, he mumbled a few words and, after turning aimlessly around the room, left. Soon the *britchka* was heard driving off.

Everyone in the room came to life. The clerk flung the pen away with an oath. The village elder and the other man both straightened out, raised their heads and waved their hands at the street as if to say: "Good riddance and don't bother coming back!" The village elder caught his breath and, combing his hair with his five fingers, exclaimed, "Well, there's a chief of police for you!"

After I told them of my misfortunes, the gentiles advised me to go to the village inn not far from there. There would be a crowd of people there on their way home from the market. Maybe one of them would be able to help me. I picked up my curl, hid it in my pocket, covered my naked cheek with a kerchief and bid them all a good night.

IX

THE INN WAS SURROUNDED BY WAGONS AND CARTS OF ALL
sorts. Some were empty except for straw. Others were
full of wares and stuff which had been bought at or left
over from the market that day. On one cart a pig lay in a
sack, his handsome snout poked through a hole, and
squealed so shrilly that my skin crawled. Behind a wagon
full of new puttees and new clay tubs and pots, a one-
horned spotted cow was struggling with all her might to
free herself from her rope. She wanted to rejoin her girl
friends in the barn with the good tidings, "It's not so
easy to get rid of me, praise the Great Wild Bull! I'm
back again and in the best of health!"

A pair of gray, broad-boned oxen stood in their yoke
and chewed their cud earnestly—they didn't waste a moment. It almost looked like they were thinking deep
thoughts and arriving at important conclusions. The inn-
keeper's goat was on top of a wagon. He poked his head
into a sack and pulled it out with a full mouth. He
snorted, swished his tail, and swiftly glanced in all directions with a quivering beard. An old, scrawny village
hound with a lame leg and clump of matted hair dangling
at the end of his tail edged his way toward the wagon,
looked up with great respect, came a bit closer, sniffed
and smelled until his nose found a dried-up bone. Seizing
the bargain, he limped away a few paces and lay down to
crack the bone, resting his head on its side as he held the
bone in his paws.

A horse hitched to another wagon, bored with standing in one place with nothing to do except to nap and wiggle his ears, decided to pay a visit to a pair of young oxen in a yoke, who were doing themselves proud over an open sack of grain, and decided to be their guest for supper. On the way, however, a wheel hub from his wagon caught the wheel of another wagon and almost upset it. The other horse, in fright, jumped out of his traces and kicked a neighboring horse who reared on his hind legs with a whinny. The terrified goat jumped off the wagon and landed on the old dog's tail. The poor old dog ran off on three legs howling at the top of his lungs.

With much effort, I fought my way through the maze of vehicles and, after looking around carefully to see if our two horses were here, I entered the inn.

I became conscious of what was going on inside only piecemeal—not all at once, but rather in successive waves. The first greeting I received was directed at my nose. As soon as I entered, that poor organ was assaulted by a sharp, bitter, overpowering stench of brandy, tobacco smoke and sweat all mixed into one. My nose promptly returned the greeting with a resounding sneeze while my ears awaited their turn. They were welcomed by a din of shrill and piping, deep and hoarse, blaring and bellowing voices which rolled in on them with deafening effect. My nose and ears having been duly saluted, the next in order were my eyes. At first they wandered about aimlessly in the murk. Later, a dense crowd of people emerged, but individual features could not yet be distinguished. At last, at the far end of the room, on a long wooden table, a wax candle in a clay pot became visible. It burned with a glaring red flame encircled by halos of yellow, green and blue which danced in the clouds of steam and columns of smoke which filled the room. Only now did beards, goatees, stubbles, whole faces and features of males and females come swimming out of the murk. Little groups of people came into view. Those who were still on their feet were only on their fourth or fifth drink.

Off to a side, two drunks were hugging each other and calling each other foul names from sheer love. Near them stood a barefoot wife in a short skirt and patched low-cut blouse. She enjoyed the scene and good-naturedly slapped each one on the back alternately, laughing, "Enough, enough, go home!" And the pair of them simply melted from love and, hugging each other even more tightly, collapsed in a heap.

Some of the customers sat on long benches at tables with bottles of brandy and food. Two fat peasants drank to each other's health and were, as the saying goes, mellow and merry. Another one, a lover of the bitter drop, who had found himself a home here in the inn, puffed on his little pipe and called to the first peasant and then to the second and then to anyone at random: "To your health! To your health!" But nobody paid any attention to him.

The last figure to swim out of the fog was that of a woman, lively, strong, with fuzzy beauty marks on her face and some sort of kerchief over her head—the innkeeper's wife, in all her glory! She flitted among the barrels, bottles, baskets, glasses, rings of bagels, boiled eggs, lean, dry fish and pieces of hard liver. Her mouth did not close for a moment. Her hands did not rest for an instant. She complained without cease. She took cash from one, security from another, and kept accounts for others by marking crosses and circles on a board with a piece of chalk.

I wandered about in this crowd like a lost soul. I tried talking to various people but the result was, as Alter used to say, "In short, nothing!"

Finally, the crowd began to thin out. Folks began to leave for home. I made my way toward the innkeeper's wife, with my whip under my arm and pointed directly at her. I did this on purpose, for I had an ulterior motive: innkeepers in general like coach drivers, and will bribe them with brandy and food so that they will bring their passengers to the inn. My whip was to be my guardian angel and endow me with grace and charm in this lady's eyes. A conversation sprung up between us:

"Good evening!"

"A good year to you!"

"Tell me, please, where is your husband?"

"What do you need him for?"

"Just like that. No particular reason."

"Tell me. Maybe I can help you."

"*Ta.* . . . Well, all right."

And so, a word here and a word there, and I told her my troubles and about the ugly situation in which I now found myself. She supported her head on her hand with two fingers extended along her cheek and sighed in sympathy as she listened: "Oh my! How terrible!"

To please her, I told her about myself: who I was, what I did for a living. She, in turn, drowned me in a torrent of talk. She told me her troubles in great detail—about her ne'er-do-well husband, her children, and the inn. A close acquaintance quickly sprang up between us. It even turned out that we were distant relatives! She was called

Chaya-Traina after a grandaunt of mine on my grand-mother's side. What a joy, what happiness! She asked about my wife, my children and each of my relatives. When her husband arrived, she quickly informed him:

"We have a guest . . . a dear guest, Reb Mendele Mocher Seforim! A relative of mine!" Then, she placed her hands on her hips, and talked condescendingly to him:

"So! You thought you took me out of a barn, did you? Don't you worry! I don't have to be ashamed, praise the Lord, before anyone. You might begin to appreciate what a family I come from!"

"*Ta!* Lord of Nations!" I said to myself. "Saul went forth to seek his asses and found himself a kingdom. I went forth to seek my horses and found myself a Chaya-Traina . . . !"

Chaya-Traina's husband was a man with a long nose; his thin beard, his side curls and eyebrows—blond as flax. When he wasn't talking, he chewed his tongue. When he was readying himself to talk, he first licked his lips thoroughly, looking, for all the world, as clever as a sheep. Upon giving me his hand by way of greeting, he mumbled unintelligibly and his whole appearance bespoke the fact that he lay firmly under his wife's heel, that he trembled at the sight of her. I later found out that in these parts he was known as Chaim-Chena Chaya-Traina's, and Chaya-Traina herself was called Chaya-Traina the Cossack.

"Where have you been loafing till now?" Chaya-Traina began to cross-examine him. "Where did the devil carry you off to, *shlimmazel?* Who ever heard of such a thing? To neglect house and home and to disappear. Don't worry! Reb Mendele is a relative. He ought to know what

77

a scourge you are, a plague that His Holy Name has saddled on me. Just look at him! Stands there like a clay statue and chews his tongue!"

"Didn't you yourself send me to Gavrilo for a sack of potatoes, didn't you?" Chaim-Chena defended himself, first licking his lips thoroughly.

"And the *Rebbe,* that handsome *Rebbe,* what's the matter with him? Is he too weak to bring the sack of potatoes? He's not too weak to eat enough for ten!"

"The *Rebbe* took the cows and the calf out to pasture, the *Rebbe* did," Chaim-Chena tried to explain to his wife.

"Oh, keep quiet! Better keep quiet and chew your tongue!" Chaya-Traina said impatiently, glaring angrily at her husband. Then she turned to me and complained about the troubles she had with each and every member of her family. Were it not for her, everything would have gone to pot long ago. She repeatedly interrupted herself with, "I don't mind if you know, Reb Mendele! To you I can talk like to a father, you're a relative."

I attempted to make peace in the family and to raise Chaim-Chena in his wife's esteem. To accomplish this, I lied a little, decried all men in general, myself included, and praised and extolled women and Chaya-Traina in particular. If, God forbid, they did not exist, life just wouldn't be worth living. Chaya-Traina softened.

"May your health prosper, Reb Mendele!" She beamed at me with a glowing face. Then she turned to her husband and spoke to him more gently.

"Enough of that tongue chewing, Chaim-Chena! Why don't you wipe the dishes and the glasses which *Esau* used instead? Reb Mendele is probably very hungry," she said, turning to me and rising from her seat at the bar.

"I'm hungry myself. We always have supper late on a market day. There's never any time. Come, please. We'd like you to come into our house."

Two dark little rooms led from the barroom to a rather large room with a low ceiling, no floor and tiny windows. Some of the panes were cracked, some patched with pieces of greased paper, and some were missing almost entirely—with only a triangle of glass left in a corner like the last tooth of an old woman. The slightest breeze made it rattle and hum a sad little tune—zim, zim, zim. In a corner of the room stood a table with long, narrow, unpainted benches next to it. The bed in the opposite corner was piled high with bedding, may the Evil Eye not harm it: pillows—large, middling, small and tiny—in a tower which reached to the ceiling. Next to the stove stood a broad bench which was used as a bed at night. On the walls hung portraits covered with cobwebs, dead flies, dried cockroach eggs, and flyspecks. From underneath the covering of filth peculiar figures peered out: a wailing wall with rabbits and fantastic animals which looked like half goat and half deer or half lion and half donkey or half leopard and half bird. A tall Haman, in a Russian Army officer's uniform, hung on a noose which barely reached his shoulders so that it looked more like the noose hung on him! Nearby stood Mordecai in a fur cap and threadbare capote tied around his waist with a rope. With his shoes, stockings and prayer curls he looked like a Jew from any small Russian town. Napoleon was there, too. He had also fallen into Jewish hands, poor man, Lord have mercy on his sad condition! His portrait hung between a small, greasy, warped mirror, on one side and Potiphar's wife on the other, a hideous creature who was flirting with Joseph and tugging at his coattails.

79

A broad, chubby, hard-working girl, with a pair of cheeks like dumplings, moved about the room. She had little hair on her head and two short pigtails behind. She kept her elbows pressed close to her sides. Both her forearms were thrust forward like two wagon shafts between which she moved. She glided along without lifting her feet, her head leading the way. She brought out a tablecloth and dishes, and began to set the table quickly. Chaya-Traina whispered something in her ear: she turned the shafts around, thrust her head forward, her body following directly behind it, and disappeared from the room.

In a corner, four children were quarreling over a little pug dog which pierced the air with its shrill cries. Chaya-Traina fell on them without warning, silently pinched one, tweaked another, and flung the puppy out of the room. The children thumbed their noses at each other and separated into different corners.

Chaim-Chena arrived with a big jug of sour cream. His wife took it and, after fussing with it for a while, asked us to wash.

A barefoot boy, in a sweater and a pair of tattered trousers, dashed in; the *Rebbe* had caught a little sparrow in the barn! The children craned their necks and gaped. Before they had a chance to recover, a young man with a somewhat swollen nose and thick lips stepped in, washed himself quickly over the pail of slops, sat down at the table, shoved a big piece of bread into his mouth and began chewing in haste, without looking around at anyone, as though fearing that the food would be gone before he could get at it. In the meanwhile, the chubby girl, the one with the dumpling cheeks, glided in again decked out in her best Sabbath clothes and also sat down at the table.

Chaya-Traina advised me, pointing a finger at the girl: "That's my oldest daughter, Chasya-Gruna!"

The company ate, mannerly at first—ladling out the soup and laying down the spoon each time—but soon the tempo increased and the din grew louder. Ten spoons dipped industriously into one bowl and flew swiftly back into ten mouths which sucked up the contents, each in its own fashion. The spoons hurried and skurried, the mouths sipped and sucked: "Whoof-hoof, hoof-foof!" My newly found relatives urged me on: "Eat! Don't wait for invitations!" And I: "Wiff-hiff!" in my own style.

The young man with the swollen nose didn't have a moment to lose; he worked for ten until he ladled his way down to the bird which was painted on the bottom of the bowl. Having finished his labors, he sighed from the depths of his belly and turned a pair of glassy eyes on the rest of the company. Then, suddenly, rising slightly from his seat, his hand shot forth toward me, accompanied by: "*Sholem aleichem!* You look familiar to me. . . . What is your name?"

I told him and he actually jumped up in surprise.

"Reb Mendele! Reb Mendele Mocher Seforim! Pish! What do you mean, who hasn't heard of Reb Mendele? Why, I had the privilege of buying a little prayer book from you in Glupsk some time ago."

"Reb Mendele is my relative," said Chaya-Traina haughtily, ready to burst with pride. Then, pointing at the young man, she informed me: "That's our *Rebbe!*" Turning to the barefoot boy in tattered trousers, she said, "Now, Sheekeleh, Reb Mendele will hear you say your lessons. Don't be ashamed, he won't eat you!"

Sheekeleh, with a finger in his nose, looked away and mumbled, "I'm assamed to, I'm assamed to. . . ."

"How old is your Sheekeleh, may he live long?" I asked the mother.

"My Sheekeleh, may he live long, was *bar mitzvahed* this past spring," answered the beaming mother.

"Well now, Sheekeleh," I said, gently pinching the boy's cheek, "tell me, and don't be ashamed, which *sidra* is being read in the synagogue this week?"

"Go ahead, go ahead!" Sheekeleh was urged from all sides.

He stared blankly and said nothing.

"B . . . b . . . b . . ." The *Rebbe* hinted with his thick lips.

"B . . . b . . . bull!" exclaimed Sheekeleh looking to the *Rebbe*.

"Well, Balak, Balak . . ." I prompted him and questioned him further: "And what did Balak say to the elders?"

The *Rebbe* licked his finger in order to give his pupil a hint.

"To lick!" shouted Sheekeleh with enthusiasm.

"Who, who?" the *Rebbe* urged him on, believing that his pupil was on the right track. "Who, eh?"

"The *Rebbe!*" Sheekeleh cried.

"Oh, you clogged head!" the angry *Rebbe* exclaimed with heat. "Who, did Balak say, will lick?"

"The Jews!" answered Sheekeleh quickly with a shriek.

"The Jews, the Jews . . . Sheekeleh!" I said, patting his cheek. "Very good. You know your lessons."

The mother did not know what to do with herself for joy. She folded her hands over her belly and said with a face all aglow: "Blessed be the belly that bore such a gem!" The father chewed his tongue and was immensely pleased.

After supper, Chaya-Traina suggested the following plan to me: "In a couple of hours, my worker Yanko will arrive with the horses. You, Reb Mendele, will ride one and my husband the other and you will bring the wagons and the wares here. And then we will decide what else to do. In the meanwhile, lie down and rest. Here is a freshly made bed for you."

"Thank you kindly!" I said. "But I'm afraid that if I crawl into that soft bed, it will be hard to get me out. God knows how long I can sleep there, and every moment is dear to me now. Some other time, God willing, I'll come to visit with my wife and children. Then, you will see, I will place myself in His hands and plunge into that pile of softness and stay there for a long, long time!"

"We want you to come, we do!" Chaya-Traina said winningly. "And remember to bring all the children. And bring Yachna-Sossa too! But don't refuse to take a little pillow, at least, into the little room with you. Sleep well," she said. "Don't worry about a thing. I'll wake you early, at the crack of dawn."

X

CHAYA-TRAINA WAS INDEED A PIOUS JEWESS AND A GOOD woman, but the bedbugs in her house were positive villains. They attacked as soon as I lay down on the sofa in the little room, and war broke out between us. Both sides were determined and fought valiantly; they with their mouths, I with my hands. They advanced, and I jumped up; they bit and I scratched; they drove ahead, and I retreated into the pillow. Finally I flung the pillow aside—the devil take it—but it struck a three-legged stool which toppled over smashing the clay water pitcher with a crash. Frightened cockroaches scurried over the floor in confusion. Feathers from the torn pillow flew about, into my nose and into my eyes. The sofa under me creaked and squeaked. The biting did not cease for a moment, nor did my twisting and turning. The stench of bedbugs was overpowering. At last, disgusted by the whole business, I decided to give it up. I sprang off the sofa and made for the window to catch a breath of fresh air. God's world spread out before me.

The golden moon sailed calmly across the dark blue sky. Her bright face was deep in thought. All was quiet around and about. . . . Her thoughtfulness cast a spell of sweet melancholy over me. Somehow she spoke directly to my heart and each glance of hers pierced my very soul. She stirred up a sea of emotions within me. My thoughts were inclined to dwell on myself—thoughts about my bitter life with its fill of illness, humiliations,

84

insults and injuries, both old and new. I whimpered like a weak child before its mother: "*Oy*, Mama! My heart is black and blue. Haven't I had my share of headaches and bellyaches? Why, then, am I in everyone's way? Haven't I had wounds enough already? Then why do they begrudge me a little peace and quiet? *Oy*, it burns! *Oy*, it hurts!"

The moon's shining face gazed down on me earnestly, intently. She looked so comforting: "*Sha*, poor child, *sha!* It can't be helped. . . ." My heart wept even more. My eyes filled with tears. I lay my head down on my arm, the side with the shorn side curl facing the moon: "Here, look! See what they've done to me!" A well of pent-up feelings opened within me, roared into my heart and flooded my mind. I stared blankly into the void with my swollen eyes and begged: "*G'vald!* Help me! Have mercy! It hurts so. . . ." That's how a sick child wakes up at night, wailing to himself, seeking help with its poor little eyes. And there is nobody! Nobody! No one hears a thing. Everyone is asleep, quiet. . . . Only a dog down the street, with his tail between his legs and his head thrown back, was awake and howled gloomily at the moon. But she sailed her course placidly, rapt in thought. There was no reason to get excited over a dog's yelping.

The weight lifted from my heart. Something warm stirred within me, a wordless feeling of hope and cheer. Just such a feeling enters a Jew's soul after he has laid his troubles before God and has cried his eyes out over them! It is a feeling which makes a man soft as dough, good without limit, glad to do anything for anybody, ready to embrace the entire world and kiss it—so overwhelming are his feelings of love.

And the little bedbugs, aren't they God's creatures?

85

Is it their fault, poor things, that they stink? Can they help it if it is their nature to bite? They don't do so out of spite or evil intent. It is only their way of earning a living—to drink, to fill themselves with someone else's blood. Goodness! This was not the first time in my life that I'd had to deal with bedbugs! Where is the Jew who can't count his dealings with them in the hundreds, nay, in the thousands?

It was with great effort that I rose the next morning. Every bone in my body ached. But Necessity drove me and raised me from my place of rest. A Jew lives in haste. It is Necessity that drives him to it, forces him to run and chase about, to hustle and bustle. He only has to slow down a trifle and he collapses like a sack of flour. It is during holidays that a Jew becomes aware of all his aches and pains. Only then does he have enough time to be sick.

Necessity raised me from my berth; Necessity kept me on my feet; Necessity sat me on a horse and gave me a jolt that sent me off at a gallop together with Chaim-Chena, Chaya-Traina's husband. It is only the first move that is hard for a Jew. Once he is in motion, the spring needs very little winding to keep him bobbing up and down as long as need be. As a matter of fact, he may continue his motions even after he should have stopped, even after—but that's not my point. I soon regained my strength and felt hale and hearty again.

There is reason in the popular saying: "A Jewish soul cannot be fathomed." I had been under the impression all along that Chaya-Traina was so pleased with me simply because she had discovered a relative, and one, no less, who was associated with books! Being associated with anything or anyone in itself carries much weight with

Jews. Take our respectable bigwigs, for example. Whenever they have any business to transact in the government offices, they start first with the janitor of the building. After all, being associated with officials, as he is, some of their grandeur rubs off on him. So they talk matters over with him and go away happy. "That should do for the time being," they say to themselves. "After all, the janitor isn't a bad fellow."

Hence a janitor of a government school for Jews is known as "the inspector"; a Jew who delivers letters is a "post office official"; and a Jew who works in the post office proper is a "postmaster." Small wonder, then, that we have a saying: "The Rabbi's gentile scrub woman can also interpret the *Torah*."

While we were having supper, I noticed that the broad, chubby girl was all dressed up—obviously a girl for whom it was high time to get married—and I began to suspect that Chaya-Traina's joy meant that I would be of use to her in making a match for her daughter. I suspected further that she had her eye on me proper. That was why the girl had her best clothes on. My suspicions were confirmed by Chaim-Chena's conversation as we rode along. He was far too interested in my son:

"So! Your boy was *bar mitzvahed,* was he, and he isn't engaged to anyone, is he? When I was his age, I was married already, I was . . . my Chaya-Traina doesn't let me sleep at night, she doesn't: '*G'vald,* find her a husband! How can you sleep there like that? What kind of father are you!' You saw my girl, didn't you? A good housekeeper, she is. Maybe it's time for her to be married, maybe. You're a scholarly man. Tell me, is it time? My wife talked to me about it last night. She thinks very highly of you, she does. . . . Things always happen unexpectedly. It just had to happen that you should wander into our house. So your son was *bar mitzvahed,* your son was?"

While we were conversing this way, we arrived at the field where the two wagons stood. First, I made sure that my wagon was intact. Then I looked at Alter's wagon. It stood in the same place and seemed to be in order. I lifted the canvas cover of the wagon to check the contents. But hardly had I put my hand in, when I froze in horror. Something was moving inside. I jumped away in fright. The canvas lifted, and sitting bolt upright before me with a bandaged head was—Alter Yaknehoz.

XI

WHAT HAD HAPPENED TO ALTER, WHERE HE HAD BEEN, HOW he had returned, why his head was bandaged—all these questions were soon answered for us by Alter in his own way:

"Well, I started out after the horses. In short, no horses! I thought to myself that they must have wandered a good way off. The grass in the woods is very good and there is plenty of shade there, so why not? A human being, forgive the comparison, would also wander a good way off in search of something good. Well, I walked further and further, if you know what I mean. But there was neither sight nor sound of them. I didn't know what to do. A nasty situation! Suddenly, I thought I heard something on the other side of the valley. Without a second thought, I went down one side and up the other. I looked here, I looked there, in short—nothing. Meanwhile it was getting late. It was dark in the woods—a bad business! Again I thought I heard a sound. I started off after it, wandered around, looked, searched—again, nothing. I was getting annoyed. What was going on here? Again a sound and something like steps.

" 'Now I've got them, the fine fellows! May they break their bones!' I cursed in anger and worked my way toward the sounds. After much effort, I finally came to a forsaken spot with thick, tangled branches. Aha! Here it is! And what do you think it was? A red cow, the devil take her—

a cow that must have strayed from the herd and got herself lost in the forest.

"What next? I didn't know where I was and there was no point in standing here. Well, I put myself in God's hands and started walking again. I stumbled along until I came across the smoldering remains of a campfire. Potatoes were still smoking in the ashes. Many feet must have walked on the grass around the fire. All around were bread crusts, eggshells, skins of cucumbers, onions and garlic, and shreds of cloth and rags. There must have been quite a company here, probably gypsies. Not a good sign at all—gypsies like to steal.

"Suddenly, I thought I heard someone calling. The first thought in my mind was, 'Maybe it's Reb Mendele!' and I hurried toward the voice. The closer I got to it, the more terrible it sounded, as if someone were crying, 'Help! *G'vald!*' I was scared, but in short—nothing! I wasn't going to stop now. I took good care to look around in case there should be trouble. In short, a little inn appeared—a hovel on shaky legs. There was something I didn't like about the whole business. I hid off to a side among some bushes. My hand found a stick. I grabbed it, if you know what I mean. It might come in handy as a weapon. I sat there and waited to see what would happen. Horrible thoughts occurred to me; I remembered tales about the Glupsk bandits and robbers.

"Suddenly, another scream, a bitter cry from someone in great distress. And it came right from the hovel! My heart leaped. Before I knew what I was up to, I was out of the bushes and standing next to the little inn. I don't even know how I got there. A thought pecked away at me: 'Maybe it's Reb Mendele who is in trouble?' I had no idea where I was, but I had to find out what was going on in there if it was the last thing I did. You know, I'm sort of a stubborn mule myself.

"In short, I moved slowly and listened carefully. I could hear a muffled cry. I came upon a crumbling stone wall which could barely stand up, it was so old. I slipped in on tiptoe and looked, trying to see in the darkness. There was a deadly silence. I took a pack of matches out of my pocket. I rubbed and rubbed; but it was no use. My hand shook and they wouldn't light. Finally the last one flared up for a minute, long enough for me to hear the cry again from a corner of the room. Then the match went out. I felt my way in the darkness and stumbled on a body. I tell you, my hair stood on end.

"In short, the light of the rising moon came in through a broken window and showed a moldy little room without a door, with someone lying, tied like a sheep, both hands and feet—half dead, white as a sheet, and barely breathing.

" 'God himself must have sent you here!' he exclaimed. 'Cut me loose right away, or I'm done for. The rope has cut into my hands and I feel like I'm on fire. I need a drink!'

" 'Who tied you up like that?' I asked and, taking out my knife, cut the ropes.

" 'The devil take his father's fathers!' he swore and straightened out. 'The bastard! Notke the Thief!'

" 'What, a thief?' I cried and looked sharply at the fellow.

" 'Yes, yes! A thief! He just stole two horses today.'

"I almost jumped when I heard this. In short, I questioned him about the details. I described our horses and soon it was all clear as day. It turned out that a whole band of tramps had camped at that fire in the woods. One of them went for a walk in the woods and came back with our horses. As soon as I found out which road they had taken, I wanted to go after them without wasting any time. The fellow tried to talk me out of it. He threw cold water on my plan. He knew this bastard—he was a murderer and was traveling with several vans full of tramps no better than he. But I couldn't rest. I couldn't be without a horse. No, no! I had to catch them, come what may. No one was going to make a fool of me! Every second was dear now.

" 'You wait here for me,' I told him. 'Rest up. When I come back with the horses, with God's help, we'll both go away from here together.' That's what I told him. He attracted me for some strange reason. Then I set out after them as fast as I could.

"That ruined old inn in the woods was near the cross-road on the highway. The road to the left went to Glupsk, to the Volhynia; to the right, the towns of Podolya. In short, I didn't walk, I ran. I was so angry that it hurt. I could have torn that thief to pieces like a herring. I needed only this to round out my luck—to be stuck in a field without a horse and without a groschen in my pocket. But nothing! Soon my feet began to complain. I was walking too fast. Then my stomach began to demand food—it just wouldn't listen to reason. This was no laughing matter! We had fasted all day.

"One thought plagued me: that this was thrown-out work, that my running was in vain! Those fine creatures had a head start. Besides, they were riding and I was on foot. My only hope was that a wagon going my way would overtake me. Luckily, the moon was full so that it was almost as bright as day. In short, I kept right on, not as fast as before, not as eagerly as before, but onward I went

anyway. There wasn't a living soul in sight. But, nothing!
I kept at it, and walked on and on. When I decide to do
something, I don't quit so easily, if you know what I mean.
In short, I thought I heard the sound of wheels. . . .
Damn it! They were coming toward me, instead of going
my way! *Ai,* what luck, what miserable luck!

"I appealed to one driver and to another. They were
all as drunk as Lot. I was bursting with anger, if you
know what I mean! I started off again at double speed.
I had already walked a long way and it was very late. I
still hoped that a wagon going my way would catch up
with me and help me. Up ahead, I thought I saw some
wagons, but the devil take it! Again the wrong way! 'No,'
I thought, 'this time I won't let them pass so easily. I'll
give them whatever I have and make them take me my
way.' I walked toward them, feeling brave, but it seemed
that they weren't moving. They were standing still.

"What a heartache! What cursed luck! But, nothing.
In short, coming closer, I saw that they were vans. It occurred to me immediately that maybe this was just what
I was looking for. I slowed down, walked quietly, cautiously, and thought, 'What shall I do now?' A little wood
stood at the side of the road. I ducked in and hid among
the trees. From there I could look the vans over closely.
Yes, they fitted the description in all details. It was they!
One van lay on its side surrounded by a crowd: men,
women—young and old—children, in rags and tatters.
One was chopping, another was banging, a third one was
offering advice, and still another was swearing and cursing. Women were screaming and children whining. It
was a cursing, a growling, a slapping, a groaning, a crying
and a laughing all mixed into one.

"Shouts pierced the air: 'It's all because of that new

93

horse, he should burn in the fires of hell!' or 'What a cripple! He kept on pulling to one side all the way, as if for spite. He should drop dead!' One of them, a redheaded broad-shouldered thief, cried, 'It's another one of Notke's bargains, the cholera take him! He only brings us mouths to feed, stink pots, bundles of straw without feet, without eyes, without anything—just bellies to stuff!' and he stomped around waving his fist at everybody.

"I looked around and what do you think I saw? Reb Mendele! Your horse! Behind the last van, he stood unharnessed, with traces trailing on the ground. They gave him the honor of riding free, without a load. 'Ah, my sage.' I was overjoyed. 'You've created a real commotion here! Good boy! And where is my wretched beast? There she is, tied up behind the same van.' Taking out my knife, I tiptoed to the van, quiet as a kitten, while the whole company was busy at the axle of the other van. I swiftly cut the ropes, leaped up on mine bareback, and without any farewells rode off with both horses. But, nothing! One of the bunch, the devil take him, had to see me and give the alarm. The redheaded thief rushed after me pell-mell and tried to overtake me. But I didn't spare the whip and drove the horses as fast as I could. This time they did not wait for invitations and galloped for all they were worth. I left the redhead far behind. But, you need luck, if you know what I mean. My mare tripped in the traces dangling behind your horse—I was in such a hurry that I didn't remove them. She fell, and in no time at all the redhead was on top of me and flung himself at me like a wild animal. We wrestled in silence with all our might. We were both in such a rage we couldn't talk. We tried to throw each other down but we both fell. We held each other in such a tight grip that our bones cracked. In short,

94

we both worked hard. One minute I was on top of him and he squeezed so hard I thought the devil would take him: The next minute, the tables turned; he was on top of me and I was underneath. But, nothing! I gave it to him good, if you know what I mean. He twitched and lay there like dead. This was only a feint. I let go but, that was just what he was waiting for. He fussed quietly and pulled a knife out of his pocket.

" 'Ha! So that's the kind you are!' I shouted and gave him a crack on the hand so that the knife flew far away. With all his strength, he leaped at me, nimble as a cat, and grabbed my throat. He might have choked me, but just then the tinkling of a bell could be heard in the distance. He was frightened. After all, he was a thief. 'It's your filthy luck!' he growled like a bear. 'Here's a present from me!' He gave me a wallop on the head and disappeared. I got up, jumped on the horse and was off again. Later I began to feel the pain. I touched my head —*beh,* a big bump on my forehead! But, nothing. I did what I'd set out to do, if you know what I mean. I had the horses!"

"Praise the Lord that you got away alive!" I exclaimed and hugged Alter for joy.

"That's nothing," said Alter. "Let that redhead praise the Lord that he came upon me after I'd been fasting for twenty-four hours straight and was all tired out. But our horses are here."

"Where are they, our lions?" I inquired, looking all around.

"Take your time, Reb Mendele," Alter answered. "The fellow I came back with is watering them. I came back myself just a little while ago. I was tired and aching, may it not happen to you, so I lay down in the van to take a nap and covered myself with the canvas. I had just closed my eyes when you arrived, Reb Mendele, and praise God, you are well. Why is your cheek bound, Reb Mendele? A toothache, eh?"

"Your head is bound, Reb Alter, because you have a bump, and mine—because I'm missing a side curl. You brought your fellow and I brought Reb Chaim-Chena Chaya-Traina's husband!" I introduced him for the second time with his complete title.

Alter stared at me inquiringly.

"What do you mean?" I asked in wonder. "You don't know Chaya-Traina?"

"Well, Chaya-Traina is Chaya-Traina," Alter wondered in turn, "but the side curl, what does that have to do with the side curl?"

"A relative. My wife is a relative," Chaim-Chena explained doltishly.

As we conversed, sitting there on the grass, our lions appeared in the distance, bumping up and down and acting as if they were galloping. They looked different to me, somehow, since yesterday. Their heads were thrown back proudly, as if to say: "Go ahead, laugh at the way we gallop! Still, there was someone who wanted us, who wanted us badly enough to steal us. Yes! Even with one leg bandaged in rags and a festering eye! Yet, we still know how to run free behind a wagon. And when it comes to breaking axles, we know how to do that too—as well as anyone else. It's our misfortune that we are Jewish! You, Reb Jews, know how to promise food to your horses, but who can live on promises?"

I slapped my horse's chin lovingly as he came up to me and chuckled to him, "You rascal, you."

Right behind the horses came the fellow Alter had

96

brought. I took one look, clapped my hands, and shouted:

"Fishke! Speak of the devil and there he is!"

"The same Fishke? The one you were telling me about?" asked Reb Alter with great wonder.

"Yes, the very one. The one from the bathhouse. Well, *sholem aleichem*, Fishke!"

"And I recognized you too, Reb Mendele," said Fishke and shook my hand.

"We owe thanks to your Fishke, Reb Mendele," said Alter to me. "If not for him, we would have seen our horses again like we'll see our ears."

"And if not for Reb Alter"—Fishke turned to me also —"Fishke would have been a dead duck by now."

"So I heard," I said. "But tell me, Fishke, how do you come to be here at all?"

"That's a long story," answered Fishke turning his head away.

I stood there a moment and looked closely at Fishke. The poor fellow was in rags. His bloody swollen feet were bare. He was sunburned and thin as a rail—a bag of bones. My heart wept at the sight of him. He must have had a bellyful of troubles. I took him by the hand and said:

"We'll hear your story later, Fishke. There's time enough for that. Meanwhile, rest here with us a little."

XII

HAD A TALENTED WRITER SEEN US ON THAT FINE MORNING,
he would have found ample material for a poem. This
would have been a poem about four married Jews and
how they lay unbuttoned on the grass, enjoying the day
in silence. Also included would be a sun and its warm
rays, a sky, nature, dewdrops, songbirds and horses, each
prettier than the last. Such a writer should, of course, be
generous enough to add some products of his own imagination too: a flock of sheep grazing in the meadow, a
clear running brook at which "Jews do break their thirst."
He would doubtless place flutes in our mouths on which
we would trill a song of praise to the beloved bride in
the *Song of Songs,* just like the shepherds of yore. We had
our own baskets of food, thank God, so that we would
not have to impose upon the writer for refreshments. This
far you may go, Reb Writer, but no further! You shall
not delve into *my* soul or palm off your little wisdoms by
putting them in my mouth—that is not for you. You'd
better find yourself another victim. . . . I can express
my thoughts better myself.

Nothing simpler. I lay there with my eyes open and
had a wonderful time. Why? No particular reason. I just
felt good all over. And I started humming out loud, not
for the purpose, God forbid, of giving a concert or exercis-
ing my voice, but just so—just to hum a *brim-brim, brim-
trim.* . . . Really, you can hear any Jew brim-brimming
away, without words, when the worry of making a living

has left him in peace for a while and he has nothing on his mind. Isn't that why Jews brim-trim, each to himself and in his own style, when they go strolling on a holiday, or on *Shabbes* after they've eaten their heavy *kugl*—twirling the ends of their coat belts, or twisting the tips of their beards, or clasping their hands behind their backs?

My Chaim-Chena, with beaming countenance, brimmed and trimmed also. Then, suddenly, he stood up, grasped his beard, licked his lips, and spoke:

"*Nu*, Reb Mendele! It's time, I think, time to go, eh?"

"You want to go home?" I responded and got up too. "*Nu*, then! Go, and in the best of health!"

"What do you mean?" Chaim-Chena stared at me in astonishment. "And you, Reb Mendele, aren't you coming with me? We talked about something, didn't we?"

"How can I?" I answered, pointing at my companions.

"We invite them all, all!" Chaim-Chena exclaimed. "Let them come too. My Chaya-Traina is making *varenikehs* today. There will be plenty for everybody, plenty."

"Thank you kindly." I bowed. "There really isn't time enough. There's the problem of earning a living. Give my best regards to your wife."

"God have mercy on us, Reb Mendele! My wife will murd—" Chaim-Chena wanted to say "murder me" but he caught himself and exclaimed, greatly disturbed: "My wife won't let me into the house without you. She talked the whole business over with me last night . . . you understand? You can't imagine how she is expecting you. And my daughter Chasya-Gruna, too. You understand?"

"I understand, I understand. But you must have patience. My wife will also murd—not let me into the house if I make a decision like this without talking it over with her first . . . you understand? What can I do, Reb Chaim-Chena?"

Chaim-Chena stood there as though he had been slapped. I could see that the poor man was in agony. His whole appearance showed it.

"Do me a favor and come!" he urged. "And if you really can't, then at least give me a letter, something in writing. She won't believe me alone. She'll tell me I'm a good-for-noth . . . a good-for-noth . . . she will . . . she will . . . you understand? Just write a few words. The *Rebbe* will read it to her. I beg you!"

I had no choice. It was a mission of mercy, a question of saving a soul. Although such a husband deserved to meet his fate, let me not be the agent—let him not be punished because of me. Out of my little satchel, I brought a pencil. I tore the flyleaf out of a book and sat down. Leaning back against a wagon wheel, I wrote the following words:

To the wealthy, renowned and pious lady, Chaya-Traina, may she be healthy and well, Amen!

Be it known unto you, that thanks to His Blessed Name, I am in a state of excellent health which penetrates into each and every limb of mine. May God not turn His face from us also in the future, that we may soon hear from each other, tidings of help and hope and that these tidings may find us proud, wealthy and honored, *Amen Selah,* thus be it forever. To your little children, may they live long and have many years, I send my most cordial regards, and, in particular, to your daughter, the virgin bride Chasya-Gruna, please convey my most special greetings without fail.

Further, I hereby inform you that, praise be given to His Blessed Name, the wares and the vans were found intact and in their proper place. Secondly I beg to inform you that the horses also were found. Reb Alter Yaknehoz liberated them from the hands of thieves. The blessings of our forefathers stood him in good stead in his quest. Undoubtedly, we have witnessed the occurrence of great miracles. Only we are not worthy of such benevolence from His hands. Your husband, may his light shine, will describe to you each and every detail in its particulars. Such events are indeed worthy of inscription in the Chronicles.

I beg your pardon, Chaya-Traina, as I would from my own mother, for venturing to act as a protector for your husband who, poor man, has great fright and sickness of soul because I am not returning to you today as had been agreed upon. Have mercy on him; let him not suffer a decrease in his alotted years nor any other form of punishment because I am breaking my promise and not returning with him according to agreement. It is a question of showing mercy to a living creature. He practically swooned before me; on his part, he did whatever was humanly possible. He sang praises to you and to your daughter, the bride with all possible virtue, to whom I send my most cordial regards. In brief, on his part, he did all that a husband and devoted father could possibly do . . . do you understand? And once again, do you really understand? He even tempted me with jelly dumplings and many other good things. But earning a living comes before all other things. Because one must earn his living, one must, on occasion even forego dumplings. Secondly, don't I have a spouse also? You understand what I mean, don't you? You are well versed in such matters. . . . After all, what is a man without his better half? I pray to Him that lives eternally that we shall see each other again without fail and be able to partake of jelly dumplings in a joyous mood, and maybe of *lekech* too . . . you understand? In the meanwhile, your husband must not suffer, poor man. It is a pity.

I herewith send you a gift with your husband: a new *techina* on the subject of earning a living; a *techina* for the lighting of candles; a *techina* with prayers to greet each new month; a *techina* about our ancestral mothers Sarah, Rebecca, Rachel and Leah; a brand-new *techina* for *Yom Kippur.* In addition, I am sending you a copy of the *Fountain of Clarity,* a book whose laws and precepts should be mastered and followed by each and every female. You will derive great pleasure therefrom. Your daughter, the virgin bride, will also enjoy it immensely.

Chaya-Traina! I have a request to make of you. When your bedbugs, may it not happen today, attacked and tortured me yesterday, I, in my misery, removed my woolen stockings, the ones made in Breslau, and, in my confusion, forgot them on your sofa. Find them, if you please, and let your husband wear them in good health. They are a gift from me.

Be well. Once more, convey my best regards to your little children and, in particular, to your daughter, the future bride. Do not neglect, under any conditions, to encourage and support your husband. Your husband, poor man, has a dejected and bitter look.

My whip, which I left in your little room, I leave as a gift for the *Rebbe.* He will know how to use it. Your humble servant who greets you and your little children and, in particular, your daughter, the future bride,

Mendele Mocher Seforim.

When I had read this letter aloud to Chaya-Traina's husband, he was a different man and licked his lips in delight over each new sweet turn of phrase. At several points, he slapped his forehead for sheer wonder that a person could write so well and exclaimed, "What sweet talk! Like honey, upon my word as a Jew!"

We parted in a most friendly fashion and he left with a light heart.

XIII

Since both alter and i were very tired from the pre-vious night, we decided we would sleep for a few hours. Then we would start out fresh and travel until late at night if need be. Fishke took it upon himself to watch the horses and prepare lunch.

"After what happened to me last night," he said, "I slept soundly—like after a bath. Reb Alter had a hard time waking me when he came back."

At my request, Alter lay his head on my lap. I took my knife and squeezed out the bump on his forehead with the flat of the blade. We yawned, stretched, and lay down in the shade of a tree.

Were it not for the sun which roasted us with its burn-ing rays, we would have slept until well past noon. When we opened our eyes, we found a cheerful fire blazing nearby. On it, a pot of potatoes, with an onion and a lean Jewish *kishka,* was boiling. We each took a sip of brandy and sat down with hearty appetites. We praised Fishke's cooking to the very heavens: it had the real Jewish flavor; his potatoes were fit for a king. Fishke was in ecstasy. "Eat in good health!" he wished us. "I hope you enjoy it!"

"Where, Fishke," we asked him, "did you manage to dig up a lean Jewish *kishka?* Certainly, not in either of our baskets."

"You ask where the lean Jewish *kishka* came from?" he answered. "From my basket! It so happens I was lucky

enough to hide it from that redheaded bastard, he should
drop dead!"

"Tell us what happened to you, Fishke," we asked him.

"*Ett . . .*" he sighed. "There's a lot to tell. It's a long
story."

"The day is long. We have enough time, thank God,
to hear your tale. Come, let's hitch up the horses," I said
to Alter. "We'll start on our way and Fishke will talk to
us while we ride."

When the vans were hitched up, I invited them to ride
on my wagon. But Alter invited us to ride on his. "Mine
is roomier," he said. "It's not so packed with goods."

"Well, then! Out with it, Fishke!" we said to him after
we had settled down and managed to convince our horses
to start moving. Fishke, however, was reluctant. He lowered his eyes and cracked his knuckles.

"What can I say? I'm ashamed to, somehow. I can't just
start telling! It makes me feel funny."

I encouraged him, and Alter prodded him along, in the
following fashion:

"It's only the beginning that's hard, my boy. Just say
the first word and the rest will follow by itself. I know it
from my own experience. Well, to make it short, what's
the difference? Later, you'll see yourself that it isn't so
hard. Well then, you married this blind orphan girl. *Nu,*
nothing! We know about that already. In short, what
happened after that?"

"After that? The devil take her father and his father
together!" Fishke shot out in anger. "Oh, how they took
me in!"

"*Nu, nu,* go on!" we prodded Fishke, who came to a

halt after this explosion. Fishke's mouth opened again and he continued, but with less heat than before.

"Oh, she was a wifey, she was! After we got married, we lived all right—like a Jewish couple should. I went out of my way for her. Honest, my lips should dry up if I'm lying! Every morning, I took her out to her spot at the Old Cemetery where she used to sit. She sat there and begged from the passers-by, singing a sad tune from the *Book of Lamentations*. It would have touched your heart to hear it.

"A few times a day I brought her food—something cooked or a hot bun, a sour pickle, sour milk. 'Eat, you'll feel better!' After all, she sat there all day busy making a living. Sometimes, I'd go out there just to see how she was getting along and to help out a bit. I'd give change. I'd keep track of the passers who made promises and remind her to collect from them when they came by again. Or I'd chase away cows and goats that wandered over to her and tried to eat the straw she sat on. In the month of *Elul,* I used to take her to the big fair on the outskirts of the city. She did as well as the charity hounds from the synagogue (the cantors, the sayers, the watchmen, the psalm singers, the Cabbalists, the collectors, the wick twisters, the field measurers, the weepers and the moaners). Oh children of Israel, how they milked the crowd! It wasn't hard to make a living. But once you have it good, you want it even better. When you've tasted bread, you'd like some cake.

" 'Do you know,' my wife once said to me, 'people like us will always make a living, wherever we are. In our business, to be crippled like we are is a blessing. Others with such blessings would have made a fortune by now. But we are both *shlimmazels* and don't do what we ought

106

to. Listen to your wife, Fishke. I'm a little older and more experienced than you. Take me out into the great, big world, Fishke, to far-off places. You'll see! You'll see—we'll be swimming in gold! There's nothing to do here any more. Lots of times I have to sit for a long time until someone breaks down and gives me a groschen. Everybody is talking about Lekish, the cholera groom, and his wife Pearl and how lucky they are. After they got married, they went away. Their luck, may the Evil Eye not harm them, followed right in their footsteps! Mottel the Mystic met them in Kishinev begging from house to house. Their baskets, he said, were stuffed full of all sorts of good things —hunks of challah, hominy, smoked sheep's-meat, lean *kishka,* and roast. Pearlie shines like the bright sun itself. She is fat and has a double chin, like a duchess. She won't have anything to do with Glupsk, even if they give her the whole town free.

" 'And people coming back from Odessa just can't get over the good luck that *Yontel,* the other cholera groom, has had there. They saw him riding along the main streets on his butt and God provides for him. He's doing very well there. Folks can't see enough of him! And, mind you, Odessa has enough cripples of its own, because wherever cripples are born, by and by they head for Odessa. But how can any of them compare to the cripples of Glupsk? You couldn't find cripples like the ones from Glupsk even in England! Folks say that Glupsk has a name all over the world. People come running to look at a Jew from Glupsk! I'm sure that God won't forsake us either. Let's go away, while it's still summertime. And don't dilly-dally. It's a sin to waste another day here.'

"I gave in to my wife's wheedling and we went away.

"To tell the truth, we did very well. No matter what

107

village or town we came to, we were a success. Everyone stared at us, no one turned us away. The poorhouse was always open to us for a night's rest. And houses—as many as our hearts desired. All we had to do was go from one house to another and fill our pockets, our bosoms, our baskets! For a few groschen, the *Shammes* at the Synagogue would find a place for us to stay for the Sabbath. My wife taught me the art of begging. I was very green and didn't know any of the tricks of the trade. My wife was a past master at it. She knew every trick in the books. She showed me how to come into a house, how to moan and cough and look pitiful. I learned how to beg or even demand, how to stick like a leech and bargain for more, how to bless the giver, or to swear and curse with deadly oaths. Did you think that you can just start begging from house to house? Oh, no! There's a whole science!

"To be wealthy, all a Jew needs in the beginning is luck. Later his heart becomes hard and his eyes become blind. That's to be expected. But for a Jew to be a beggar, a successful beggar, he needs more than luck. There are many things he must learn. He has to know all the tricks. He has to be able to get under someone's skin in such a way that the other fellow must give simply to get away!

"We were foot beggars, my wife and I. I see from the way you're looking at me that you don't understand. Be patient and I'll try to make it a little clearer. Beggars are divided into kinds, like soldiers. The first kind is the infantry. . . . but wait a minute, wait! There are so many kinds, hundreds of them. And I can't remember all the names. Beggars that crawl and limp and drag their feet—the devil knows what else! Beggars like flies—

tramps and idlers from everywhere, loafers, Cabbalists, plate lickers. All sorts. Let me get straightened out."

But all his thinking didn't help. Fishke was so enmeshed and entangled in his armies of beggars that he couldn't free himself. From his words, however, I made some order of the groups into which our beggars are divided. The two main ones are the *infantry*, or *foot beggars*, and the *cavalry*, or *van beggars*. The first travel on foot; the second in vans or wagons. These are further subdivided into branches: *city beggars*, those who were simply born in a city, usually in Lithuania, and *field beggars*, those who were simply born on a van in a field. Their parents and their parents' parents as far back as anyone remembers have been wandering. These are the Jewish gypsies. They wander forever from one end of the land to the other. They are born, grow up and marry, they multiply and die—all on the road. They are free people, relieved of being Temple slaves, of paying the kosher meat tax and the like. They are also rid of praying and Jewishness—they have neither Lord nor Master.

The branch of *city beggars* is further broken down into many types. There are the simple *starvelings*—men, women, girls and boys who go from house to house with their baskets on *Rosh-Chodesh* and also in the middle of the month and beg groschens and crusts of bread. Many of the boys and girls run after you in the streets and catch at your coattails until you ransom yourself by giving them something. Then, there are the *synagogue official starvelings*—the Cabbalists and the loungers who mouth the traditional saws and who say *kadish* for the dead at the Holy Resting Place. To their number may be added the *shofar* blowers, the *Mezuzah* inspectors and their ilk. Then, there are the *Torah and good-deed starvelings*—

the Pharisees who desert wife and children and bury themselves in a far-off prayer house to study the tractate *Betsa* at public expense. To this type belong the *Yeshiva* students who wander about in a bedraggled state, sit at the stove scratching themselves and eat in a different house every day. Also, those Jews who tramp about with a kerchief in hand, so-called collectors, supposedly collecting donations for this or that charity. There are *secret starvelings,* wealthy proprietors who quietly accept support and alms. There are also *semi-starvelings* such as, for example, the Talmud-Torah teachers in many cities who are semi-beggars. In this class may be included synagogue attendants, judges, and rabbis. Each of them is half —half what he is supposed to be and half what all Jews with baskets are. Then there are the *holiday starvelings.* They play the part on holidays like Purim, when Jews go from house to house in groups to celebrate the festivities. But the *holiday starvelings* claim to be collecting money for charitable purposes. And finally, there are the *loan-of-honor starvelings,* who accept alms all their lives under the pretext that it's a loan of honor. They swear that they'll return it tomorrow or the day after with thanks.

"Reb Alter," I said after I had succeeded in arranging our beggars in the above order from Fishke's description. "Reb Alter, remind me, I beg you, if you remember any other sorts of beggars whom I've forgotten, God forbid, to include in my list."

"What difference would it make?" Alter answered and looked at me like a grown man looks at a boy who is making a fool of himself. "*O-vah,* he has, God forbid, forgotten! Such an important list! And if you're not included in the list, you can't be a beggar?"

"Don't say that, Reb Alter!" I defended myself. "Our

paupers are very conscious of their dignity. They seek honor with all their might. Insult a pauper and he will remind you of it to the end of your days! *Sha!* You see? While we've been talking, I reminded myself of a whole catalog of beggars, may the Evil Eye not harm them: pilgrims to Jerusalem, Jews on their way back from Jerusalem, Jews who were burned out, sick Jews, Jews with hemorrhoids and doctors' letters to prove it, deserted wives, widows of all sorts, writers, and—the devil won't take us, Reb Alter—we might as well include book peddlers. And if that be the case, why not count in our printers and editors and all their workers, the typesetters, the proofreaders, the correspondents—let them all join the ranks of the paupers! And now, Reb Alter, we really ought to sort them all into their proper places on the list. I didn't forget anyone, did I?"

"*Ai, feh,* Reb Mendele!" Alter exclaimed irritably and began to scratch himself. "Enough of your beggars! I'm itching all over. I feel as if I'm being eaten alive by an army of fleas. As far as I'm concerned, you can cut the whole story short: all of Israel—one big pauper! And an end to this nonsense. Let Fishke finish his story and stop interrupting him. If he gets stuck and you help him out . . . that's all right, but no interruptions!"

Right from the start, Fishke was our cantor. He opened his mouth, puckered his lips and came forth with halting and choppy notes. And I? I was his understudy. I helped him in time of need and extracted the words which jammed his throat. Without my aid, it would be almost impossible to understand him. Alter simply urged him on with a "*Nu,* in short . . ." or "In short—nothing!" as one prods the cantor in the synagogue on *Shabbes* when there is a good soup and *kugl* waiting at home after the services.

XIV

"My wife and me, we bewonged to the infantwy so you can guess how swowwy we cwawwed awong, me with my sick feet—just wike cwabs," Fishke began again in his manner, unable to pronounce an "l" or an "r." His tale, with my corrections, continues:

"Little by little my wife began to scold and swear at me. She called me names and harped on my lame feet. She complained about what a complete disappointment I turned out to be, from head to toe. She had made a man of me, showed me what the world was like, earned a living for me, put me on my feet, but I didn't appreciate it and did everything I could to spite her. She acted like this rarely, so I didn't answer back. I swallowed it all and thought: 'But that is the way a wife is supposed to be. That's the way they are. A woman honors her husband with a few curses and sometimes even with a blow.' When her anger died down, we lived in peace again; once again Fishke was a good husband. She laid her hand on my shoulder and: 'Off we go, Fishke!' I walked ahead, she followed behind, and somehow we both felt good. And that's how we crept and crawled from town to town.

"It took us such a long time to reach Balta that we missed the famous fair which is known all over the world. My wife was beside herself. She acted as if she had lost a vast sum of money. I cheered her up by telling her that the houses of Balta were all still there, thank God. Wasn't that enough for us, so many houses, such a city? We shouldn't be such sinners! Before I could catch my breath, she shot out: 'Burn up, you and your houses! What's the good of a city, a mudhole, like this? Who wants it? Not I, do you hear? I'll have nothing to do with it! Drown in the mud here and choke on your city, your bloody Balta!' "

"Reb Alter, I've got it!" I shouted. "I just remembered another type of pauper: Bankers!"

"A real bargain!" said Alter and clicked his tongue. "As far as I'm concerned they're not worth a second thought!"

"I know one of them in Glupsk very well—Simchele the Merry. He carries with him a special book with a list of all the houses on which he holds mortgages and how much income he gets from each. 'The houses,' he says, 'are mine. They pay duty to me! All of Glupsk belongs to me.' Every day he goes to a different block of houses. He breezes into a house with a loud greeting. If he receives his alms promptly, then all is well. If not, he says, 'Good day! Don't you worry, I'll keep track of your debts!' and off he runs. Maybe you have heard about the beggar from Glupsk who made a match with another one from Teterivke and, as dowry, threw in half the houses of Glupsk? That was Simchele the Merry! Or, perhaps you have heard tell how, at a meal for paupers given by a wealthy man in honor of his child's marriage, a beggar who was invited arrived dragging with him another one who wasn't? When they asked, 'Uncle, how is it that you brought along another mouth to feed?' he answered, 'Oh, that's my son-in-law. I give him his room and board!' That, too, was Simchele the Merry! In short, Simchele looks upon Glupsk as his city and all its houses belong to him."

"For my part, your Simchele can drop dead," Alter commented briefly and asked Fishke to continue his story.

Fishke began again after his fashion and I helped him along after mine.

"We didn't follow any straight path. We just wandered along from city to city. Finally we came to the city of A——. *Oy,* how much better off I would've been if I'd never laid eyes on the place! It's not that I have anything against the city itself. Just the opposite—it was a good city. I went from door to door to my heart's content. But it was there that I met my Executioner, he should be slaughtered with a dull knife! His bones should rot! This is how it happened.

"The cavalry was stationed in that city—the field beggars with their vans. A revolution had just taken place there. The richer young men of the town had just started something new. They decided that it wouldn't hurt the beggars to work for their daily bread—except for the old and sick and crippled. There was no reason for healthy young men and women to live on alms and charity. The foolish Jewish spirit of charity causes only trouble, they claimed. That's why, they said, there are so many lazy loafers among the Jews—who suck other people's blood like bedbugs. The rich young men set up a sort of factory where the beggars were put to work making ropes and sewing sacks and, in return, were given food. Beggars began to turn up much less often in the town.

"The field beggars that we met there were up in arms against this new custom. '*G'vald!*' they cried. 'What's happening to the world? Where is Jewish charity? Jewishness is dead!' One of them, a redhead and strong as an ox—his bones should rot!—was the ringleader and shouted louder than anyone else. 'It's Sodom, that's what it is! Sodom all over again! Why should the rich sit around like princes, doing nothing, while others work for them?

Doesn't everything they own come from other people's toil, other people's tears and sweat? They think they're fine folks. They take care of themselves and want others to work. A rich man, the fatter he is and the bigger his belly, the more honor and respect he gets. With us it's just the opposite. A healthy beggar has to be ashamed and hide like a thief. Otherwise people raise a hue and cry and demand why such a healthy fellow isn't working. It's time for a change—let the rich try to work a bit! What's wrong with them? They're not sick.'

" 'Right, Feibushke! We are also children of Israel and just as good as they are!' The other beggars stood up for the redheaded bastard. Then, little by little, they began to walk away from the poorhouse.

"That evening, it was my luck to be walking by the courtyard of the Synagogue. It was dark and there were many people, may the Evil Eye not harm them, milling around. Off to a side, I heard someone crying so bitterly it would have moved a stone. I stopped. Not far from me stood a broken man. A little pillow lay on his two outstretched arms. A tiny baby on the pillow squealed and lost its breath in a fit of sobs. The poor father didn't know what to do. He rocked it, bounced it, tried to quiet it with a weeping voice and miserable groans: 'Oy, woe is me! Black is my lot! My wife is dying and leaving this tiny infant on my hands! Oy, woe is to you, poor little orphan! Black will be your lot without a mother! A—a—a—ah, sha, sha! What can I do for you, poor baby?'

"Everyone who passed by put something in his hand. The women tried to comfort him but he didn't stop moaning for a minute: 'Woe is me, black is your lot,' rocking the pillow and turning hopelessly with it in all directions. My heart was torn with pity for the poor father and his

116

unlucky orphan still in diapers. I took three groschens out of my pocket and went up to the poor man. I stretched my hand over the pillow to give him the money when he suddenly pinched me and cried in his wailing voice, 'Oy, woe is to *you*,' accenting the 'you' as if he meant me. I jumped aside in fear and rubbed my hand in pain. The miserable father turned to me and pushed the pillow into my hands, saying, 'That's enough for today. Come here. Hold the child a while!' I stared and couldn't believe my eyes. The little orphan, I saw, was a doll wrapped in rags, and the unfortunate father—the redheaded bastard Feibushke, his bones should rot! He did the job like a real actor! He cried and screamed and lost his breath just like a little baby.

" 'That's the way to do business with the foolish children of Israel,' he explained. 'If they won't give you alms with good will, you have to get it out of them with tricks. That's the only way. What does the rabbi, or the judge, or any of that pack of officials do? They all disguise themselves and perform tricks. They have their tricks and I, woe is me, have my little orphan. There's more than one way to milk a cow! Say amen to that, Fishke!'

"While we were staying at the poorhouse, the redheaded bastard began to sidle up to my wife. Somehow, he was very much attracted to her. Whenever she wanted something, he rushed to get it for her. He enjoyed serving her. He stayed so close to her that little by little they both became great pals. He would sit with her for hours on end talking about nothing and telling her smutty little jokes. My wife would stop her ears and act as if she didn't want to listen. And when he flattered her and told her that she was a juicy, plump, meaty woman—just the way he liked them—she scolded him and even slapped him and laughed. I also laughed, although sometimes it was a bitter little laugh, and thought, 'Why should I worry about that bag of wind? Tomorrow or the day after, we'll be rid of him. He'll go his way, we'll go ours, and I'll never have to look at his ugly mug again. Besides, when we go begging, she goes from house to house with me, praise the One Above. When he, the bastard, takes her hand and wants to lead her, she pushes him away angrily and tells him to go away: she is a married woman and has someone, thank God, to go begging with.'

"The morning after the unfortunate father act, I went begging by myself. When we got up, my wife complained that she wasn't feeling well. She yawned and stretched again and again—a good omen—so she stayed home. I felt bad myself. I had a heartburn. It was lonely going from house to house all alone that day. I was worried, too. I have to admit that after the redheaded bastard started sidling up to my wife and telling her his little jokes, she became dearer to me. Sometimes I was very angry, burning mad, but at the same time, I don't know why, I was drawn to her. It was like magic. It was like—how can I explain it—like scratching one of those itching sores that I get sometimes. It was pain and pleasure, both together. My begging somehow had a different taste that day than on other days. I made a short job of it and got it over with quickly.

"When I came back to the poorhouse, I found my wife sitting with the bastard. Both of them were whispering together. Her face was flushed. She bent her head toward him and listened to his talk with a sweet smile on her lips. When I came up to her and asked how she felt, she was caught off guard. She sat speechless for a minute and didn't know what to do. Then she stretched out her hand to touch me, as she usually did, and said, 'Do you know why I'm sick, Fishke? It's because of an Evil Eye. It's because of our dragging along on foot. The woman leech came in to see me and sent me down to the bathhouse. She told me to whip myself well and let them cup me. Then, before I go to sleep, she said I should rub myself down and work up a sweat during the night. No, Fishke! I can't go on foot any longer. Reb Feibushke here has invited us to ride with him in his van. What shall we do, Fishke? What do you say?'

"The bastard, his bones should rot, grinned at me with a look in his eye that went right through me. It cut me to the quick. I felt like a little boy when the *Rebbe* tells him to lie down on the bench for a whipping. I hemmed and hawed and couldn't put two words together.

" 'Why are you silent? Why don't you answer?' my wife shouted angrily. 'I know that you don't care a bit about my health. You want to be rid of me as soon as you can. You want to drive me to an early grave. But wait, you viper! Wait! You'll go first, you'll meet your end before me. Do you hear, Fishke with your crooked legs, I'll sweep the floor with you! You won't have a hair left on your head. I'll knock every one of your teeth out!'

"Whenever my wife opened her mouth like that, my blood froze in my veins. I stood there, angry, disgusted and beaten. God alone knows how I felt then. What could I do? I bent my head toward my wife and said, '*Sha!* Don't scream and don't get so upset. If you want to ride, we'll ride. Why not?'

" 'That's the way to talk!' my wife replied a little more softly. 'Why don't you answer when people talk to you?

Why do you stand there like a clay statue? This man is kind enough to take us along free—and you don't even say thanks! Shame on you, you low-life you!'

"What could I do? I had to say thanks to the bastard, too."

"Reb Alter, another one!" I cried out.

"What is it, Reb Mendele? Another bargain?" Alter twitted me. "Reminded yourself of another kind of pauper maybe? It's time that God granted you bigger bargains. We have enough paupers!"

"No, Reb Alter! What I mean is that we have here another Chaim-Chena who quakes and quivers before his wife. Our Fishke, I'm afraid, has probably been beaten more than once by his wife."

XV

FISHKE BEGAN AGAIN IN HIS FASHION, I WORKED AND HELPED
him along in my fashion, Alter drove us both along in his
fashion, and the story continues as follows:

"The next day, the cavalry moved out of Sodom. That's
what they called the town. They left with a clang and a
clatter, with a swearing and scolding, with a creaking and
scraping of wheels. Deadly oaths rained down on the
town: 'It should burn to the ground! The rich should
die from hunger ten times a day! They should have to
wander around the world barefoot and bareback. . . .'

"Three vans were packed to the rafters with all sorts of
creatures: men, women, young women, boys, girls, big
and small, and among them my wife and myself. Congratulations! We were promoted! We were now serving
with the cavalry.

"I must tell you, dear people, a whole new world
opened for me. At first, it was very gay to be with this
band. I saw and heard such new and wonderful things! I
couldn't even begin to tell you. They made fun of the
whole world. They would mimic and laugh at anyone who
rubbed them the wrong way. One of them would describe
in thieves' language, the tricks he played or the traps he
laid: how he had 'Borrowed a bead' (stolen a bread), or
'racked up some ringers' (stolen money), or 'lectured a
lamb' (beaten a child of a rich family). They cursed the
rich at the drop of a hat, for no particular reason, but just
so. I swear by my *talles* and *tefillin* that they hate the rich

far more than the rich hate them. What wouldn't they call a rich man: a bloodsucker, a bursting belly, a clogged head, a stone heart, a stiff neck, and the devil alone knows what other names! They considered it a *mitzvah* to swindle a rich man—and the oftener, the better. Whenever they had troubles, they cursed the rich; they wished them aches and pains, cramps and convulsions, anguish and agony, and the worst kinds of disease.

"Sometimes they jokingly called me 'The Magnate' because I often defended the rich and stood up for their honor. I had lived all my life in the bathhouse. In a way, I was brought up among the rich and, after all, I'd had dealings, with them: I had watched their clothing, brought them kettles of water or hot coals and other bathhouse needs.

"The van beggars set great store on the knack of putting on an act. They needed it for their business. Whenever it paid, these fine folks would become hunchbacked, blind, deaf or dumb, or lame. But they set even greater store on the genuine article, on undisguised cripples like my wife or me. They often said that handicaps like ours were treasures for a beggar—blessings in disguise. Handicaps like ours could bring in a lot of money. They thought even more highly of my wife's than of mine. But it was her tongue that fascinated them; it ran like a machine. When she opened her mouth, it was enough to make your hair stand on end.

"The redheaded bastard hovered over my wife. He actually clung to her. He smiled to her, he pampered her, he would have brought her birds' milk. Whenever he laid his hands on something good to eat—like cooked chickpeas, plums, apples—he brought it to her. I said to myself: 'A plague on you! Why should I care? Go ahead, pet

her, pamper her. What good will it do you? Nothing! She's
a married woman. There's no danger. . . . If it's her
blindness you're after, if you're figuring that you can
make a lot of money with a blind woman, then eat your
heart out, you dog, because my wife goes begging with
me. What can you expect to accomplish by sticking to her
when the main thing is that she goes from house to house
with me?'

"Since this was how my thoughts ran, I decided to learn
the ways of a beggar down to the last wrinkle so that my
wife would be more pleased with me. I already knew how
to walk into a house. The trick was to enter in a huff, to be
angry, to demand the alms as if it were coming to you,
to hunt down the owner of the house or his wife even if
it meant going upstairs and walking into the bedroom!
The next thing was to bargain with him. As far as bargaining went, I was a past master. The whole trick was
to grumble about anything they gave. If they gave a piece
of bread, I asked for a shirt or underwear or stockings. The
trick was always to find fault and complain. You must
never thank the giver. You must scowl and sometimes even
curse.

"But the redheaded bastard wasn't asleep either, his
bones should rot! He was thinking up ways to get rid of
me. He must have said to himself: 'Fishke, in the art of
being a beggar, you're not even fit to wash my feet. I know
the tricks of the trade eighty thousand times better than
you. And, once I've taken it into my head that I'm going
to work with your blind wife, that's the way it's going to
be. Don't worry, with God's help I'll know how to take
care of you too.'

"He hounded me until I looked worse than a stray cat.
I fell terribly in my wife's estimation. She only laughed

123

at me now. All I heard from her was: 'Split a gut! Break your neck! May worms eat you! You scoundrel, you glutton, you so-and-so!'

"The redheaded bastard, may he never rise on Judgment Day, kept on baiting me and doing me dirt until I became the laughingstock of the whole company. All the vans were picking on me now. Every minute they played another trick on me. Every instant they called me another name. They did whatever they wanted to me. I was everybody's scapegoat. When I got angry they were offended: 'Look how worked up The Magnate is! He'll have a fit in a minute!'

"Or, if I couldn't hold back my bitter tears because the blows and insults I got were more than I could stand, they would say, 'What's the occasion, Fishke? You're laughing so hard you're showing your teeth. Lookee here, folks! See how Fishke is laughing.' And then the bastard's voice would rise above the others: 'Help the poor fellow, children of Israel! Give it to him in the ribs or fix his shoulders for him—that's a sure cure for laughing. And, if that doesn't work, get hold of his hair or his ear! That will put tears in his eyes as sure as an onion. You've got to help him. You just can't let a Jew suffer like that!'

"Sometimes they threw me out of the van, and when I limped after the wagon as fast as I could and had to wiggle my hips, they clapped their hands and shouted, 'Bravo, Fishke! That's the way, Fishke, dance a little, dance! Come on, folks, look at Fishke! Look at him dance, may the Evil Eye not harm him! Look at him lifting his legs! May he dance like that at all our weddings!'

"Once someone cried out—it was the redheaded bastard, his bones should rot—'Folks! Fishke isn't lame at all! He is only acting lame and putting us all to shame, the faker! Let's try to make him stand straight. Give him a smack in the back there and you'll see how straight he'll stretch his legs!' Well, they tortured me and made my life miserable. *Oy,* how I longed for those good old days when I sat in the bathhouse like a king and lived like God in France!"

"Well, then why didn't you divorce her?" Alter interrupted Fishke's tale. "That's what divorces are for!"

"You're right," answered Fishke with a sigh. "I wish I had done it then. I would be much better off today and maybe someone else would be too. . . . I don't know what was the matter with me then. It was like being under a spell. It's shameful to admit it, but my heart was somehow attracted to my wife. No matter how much I suffered, and I went through hell, the devil himself drove me to her. Maybe I was just plain stubborn: 'If you, you bastard, want to break up my marriage and get rid of me, then, just to spite you, I'll cling to her more tightly than before.' Or, maybe it was—what's a good way to say it—just because it was that way . . . I was under a spell. I was charmed by her looks. She was healthy, chubby and firm, with a full face, not pretty but charming. There were times when I didn't know where to put myself because of all my troubles and heartaches, and I wished I was dead together with her. 'Today, today,' I would say to myself, 'it must take an end. Today I will tell her—a divorce! But as soon as I would come over to her, she would start talking to me, put her hand on my shoulder and say, 'Lead me, Fishke!' My tongue would freeze, my heart would melt a little, and I was bewitched again.

"One fine day, when I was going from house to house with my wife, I felt rather good and said to her, 'Bassia, dear soul, what is the point to this endless wandering?

125

It's not for us. In Glupsk, we both had, thank God, something of a reputation. You took me out of the bathhouse there. It's nothing to sneeze at, the stone bathhouse of Glupsk; through its doors such lions passed each week, such fine gentlemen! And you, too, were well known and respected. And now, we're wandering from town to town with these beggars. And what kind of respectability do we have, tell me?'

" 'Maybe you want to go back to Glupsk?' she flared up. 'You can go back there if you want to, Fishke. But I won't! Under any conditions! There are plenty of paupers in Glupsk today without me. Every day new paupers pop up there, and brand-new alms takers. Why, even the rich go begging there today.'

" 'It doesn't have to be Glupsk,' I answered. 'Dear soul, pick any city you like and let's settle down there. Our own town and our own rich people will bring us blessings and fortune. No wonder people say: "Every dog to his own bone." '

" 'Soon, Fishke, soon,' my wife said, slapping my back in a very friendly way. 'Let's travel just a little longer. Let's live a little and see some more of the world. It's so good and lively. Be patient with your city, Fishke. Soon!'

"This 'soon' of hers was long—no end in sight. During that time, we stopped in countless cities and I went through endless torture and agony. And all because of him, that redheaded bastard, his bones should rot. . . ."

Fishke sighed from the depths of his heart and closed his eyes. We let him catch his breath and then he continued his tale.

XVI

"NOT ONLY DID THEY CALL ME 'THE MAGNATE,' BUT THEY began calling me 'The Cabbalist' also. The bastard gave me this new title, he should drop dead! And so, everyone in the band called me 'Fishke the Cabbalist.' 'Cabbalist' was such an ugly name to them that they spat seven times whenever they said it. The way the merchants, the storekeepers, the artisans—men who compete for their daily bread—hate each other is child's play compared to the hatred of the van paupers for the city paupers and especially for the whole tribe of Cabbalists. 'Those wormy Cabbalists, lazy men from good families, trying to look like somebodies in their greasy coats,' they said with gall. 'They're like bedbugs, every house is full of them and there's no getting rid of them. They stuff their bellies every time there is a wedding feast, a circumcision, the naming of a newborn boy, a funeral. They make profits from the dead as well as from the living while we have to break our backs for a crust of bread. Those moth-eaten scholars, those lazy loafers, have taken over King David's little book of psalms and they make a living at it. If King David had known into whose hands his Book of Psalms would fall, and how these moldy maggots with their pasty faces would use it, he would never have written it.'

" 'It's no use, Bassia!' the bastard said to my wife. 'We'll never be able to do anything with your Fishke. No, no! He'll never be one of us. He is a Cabbalist from head to toe, to his last hair. Your taking him traveling and trying to show him the world won't help him one bit. He doesn't know the first thing about being a beggar. Poor thing, you'll have only bitterness and heartache from him. *Ai,* what a Bassia! If only I had such a Bassia! We would make a fortune, so help me, a fortune!'

"The bastard did everything he could to break us up and told her all sorts of cock-and-bull stories and wild tales about me. Finally, he came up with something really juicy. He told her that I was running after a girl in another van and flirting with her a lot. There was a hunchbacked girl with the band that I liked to talk to, it's true—"

"What's this? Who was she?" both Alter and I interrupted Fishke. "Come now, Fishke, out with it!"

"The girl was a total stranger to the band. She had suffered enough in her childhood, poor thing. I really used to like to sit with her and talk. We used to tell each other our troubles and pour out our hearts. More than once she cried for me as well as for herself. *Ai,* if you knew what a girl she is! If you only knew what she's been through, poor thing!" Fishke exclaimed with tears in his eyes.

We asked Fishke to tell us who the girl was and what had happened to her.

"If you really want to know," Fishke said after he had wiped his eyes with his sleeve, "and if you're not bored listening to me, I'll oblige you. I'll tell you all I know. But don't hold it against me if it doesn't come out smoothly.

"She was only a little girl when her mother brought her to Glupsk together with a sack of old clothes and bedding. Her mother left the sack with an old woman—an old witch: she must have been an employment agent. The mother used to go away with her for the whole day, leaving the child all alone and without food. The girl told me

how she once cried and screamed and begged her mother to take her along. The old witch got very angry and wouldn't hear of it: 'God forbid! No one must know about her. You'll lose your job.'

"A few days later, her mother took her along and quietly kept her in the kitchen of the wealthy house where she worked. But it didn't last long. Her mother and she soon moved to a kitchen in another house and from there to still another kitchen. Every time her mother lost her job, she treated her worse and worse.

"She knew very little about her father. Before she came to Glupsk with her mother, he was hardly ever home. He was always on the road and here, in the kitchens, she never saw him at all. She would have forgotten that she ever had a father except that her mother cursed him fifty times a day. 'May he break his head somewhere, your fine father!' she would curse. 'After all the years of hardship and heartache I had with him, he leaves me in the lurch with a ball and chain, a child, hanging around my neck—may he hang himself—and now I can't keep a job and have to choke myself and keep her in hiding. Who needs a cook with a child?'

"More than once the mistress of the house would come running into the kitchen when the meal was not just so and make a scene about the cook who skims the cream from the milk to give to her dear little daughter. But the truth was that the dear little daughter starved and wasted away with nothing to eat but her own little heart. Her mother used to stow her away, like smuggled goods, on top of the stove and there she sat in a corner all day, hunched over, not daring to move or make a sound. Her mouth watered from the kitchen smells—the roast goose and the fried livers—but she? *Sha,* not a word!

"She suffered in silence, poor thing, until someone remembered to push a dry crust of bread into her hand, or a gnawed bone or some other leftovers. But many times no one remembered to give her anything. When she couldn't stand it any more and finally made a sound, a rolling pin or a broomstick would appear on top of the stove and beat her—on the head, on the hands, on the feet, wherever it happened to strike—while deadly oaths and curses rained down upon her father and her father's fathers all the way down to Abraham, our Father. That's how she spent her childhood in sickness and suffering on top of kitchen stoves. Because she always had to sit humped over in one position, she became hunchbacked, poor thing.

"Looking down from her perch on the stove, she used to see a young man. He often came to visit her mother in the kitchen. Her mother beamed whenever he came and looked after him like the apple of her eye. She filled his pockets with good things to eat and sometimes gave him money too. He used to often come late and spend the night in the kitchen. Sometimes her mother dressed herself very carefully, looking into her little mirror, and then disappeared for the whole night. Her mother must have been getting ready to remarry and was very busy with the bridegroom. . . .

"Once, toward evening, a stranger came and took her mother's things from the kitchen. Then her mother thanked the lady of the house for the bread and salt, took her almost naked little daughter off the stove and left with her. She led her far, far away to a side street. 'Sit down here and wait. People will take pity,' her mother told her and vanished.

"The poor little castaway sat quietly on the street and

was afraid to move, just as before on top of the stove. A cold autumn drizzle soaked her to the bone. She sat there, huddled up, in her thin little dress, shivering and shaking. When a passerby asked her: 'Who are you, little girl?' she answered: 'I'm my mother's little girl . . . she told me to sit still here . . . I mustn't cry . . . a rolling pin or a broomstick will beat me.' She sat there until late at night, when some woman coaxed her home with sweet talk, way out, to the edge of town, to a little hut that was ready to fall down.

"She lived with this woman for a long time. It was no land of milk and honey for her. The woman said she was an aunt of hers and that's what she told the girl to call her. This Auntie was a market woman; she sold roasted potatoes, hot babkas, tiny wild pears, and little apples from Palestine. She used to go to the market early in the morning. The hunchbacked little girl stayed behind to rock Auntie's baby daughter, to pick up slivers of wood from the street to burn in the stove, to gather the eggs from under the chickens' roost, to scrub the dried *kasha* from the pots, to soak the baby's dirty shirts in the pail of slops, to watch the wooden *milchikeh* spoon drying in the sun together with the baby's pillow, and to do other similar chores. In the evening, when Auntie came home, she sent her little servant begging for crusts of bread from house to house. These crumbs that she gathered were her food, and what was left went to Auntie.

"One summer evening, while begging from house to house, in a coarse blouse and skirt, she strayed far to the other end of town and couldn't find her way back. The sun had set a long time ago. A black cloud covered the sky. Soon the storm broke with flashes of lightning and peals of thunder. Suddenly some vans appeared, packed full of people, on their way out of the city. 'Look! There's a hunchbacked little girl! She's crying. She must be lost!' came a cry from one of the vans. Soon, a redheaded man jumped down—the same redheaded bastard, his bones should rot—and asked her who she was. 'I want to go home, home to Auntie!' sobbed the little girl. '*Sha!* Don't cry,' the bastard said to her. 'I'll take you home to your aunt.' He swept her into the van and rode off with her.

"Since then the hunchbacked girl, poor thing, has been roaming the countryside with these van beggars. They made a living from her hump. Whenever they came into a city, they sat her out on the main street barefoot and half naked. She was supposed to sob and beg for alms, whining and pulling peoples' coattails as they passed by. Sometimes she didn't play the part with her whole heart and came back with very little. But she certainly received plenty of beatings in her van. They beat her without mercy and threw her out of the wagon, poor thing, hungry and naked, so that she had to whine and cry in earnest.

"She told me how once, during a terrible cold spell, they threw her out on the street in the middle of the night. The cold made her double up like a *bagel*; it pinched and pricked. She thought she'd go out of her mind. Light and dark flashed before her eyes. In a minute she'd die, she thought. She couldn't stand it any longer and began to cry bitterly, asking them to let her back into the house. She shivered and begged for mercy: 'Open up, Auntie, open up, Uncle!' she called to some of the band. She screamed: 'Uncle, I'll beg in earnest from now on! *G'vald!* I'll really beg well!' But it was like talking to the wall. They wouldn't answer.

"She lay down quietly. She didn't feel the cold or pain

any more, and fell into a deep sleep. It seemed to her that she was being hugged and kissed. It was so good and warm, a pleasure! And they carried her away half dead. She was sick for a long time after that.

"Another practice of theirs was to drop her off the wagon as soon as the carriage of a wealthy nobleman or a merchant appeared in the distance. She had to go through the whole performance: she had to run after the horses or alongside the carriage, with outstretched hands, and sob and whine through her nose and look pitiful. She had to come back with money if it was the last thing she did. Sometimes the coachman lashed her but she swallowed it without a sound and kept up the performance. A lash from the coachman was nothing compared to what she would get if she came back to the wagon empty-handed.

"I can't even begin to tell you what she's been through. And it's still going on today! Even in hell things can't be as bad. Oh, my blood boils when I remind myself of the way she lives! *Oy vay,* I'd give my life to free her. Listen to me, there is no one in the whole world as good and as sweet as she!"

XVII

FISHKE'S STORY CAST BOTH ALTER AND ME INTO A DEEP melancholy. Alter rubbed his forehead with his fist, as though he had an itch, and groaned to himself.

"Do you hear, Reb Alter?" I said with a little smile. "Our Fishke is really head over heels in love with the hunchbacked girl. It's strange. . . ."

"Why should I deny it?" said Fishke. "I pitied her with all my heart. I was drawn to her more and more. It did me good just to sit with her. What did we do? Nothing! We just sat and talked or looked at each other without talking. Goodness was written all over her face. She looked at me as only a devoted sister looks at her brother when he's in misery. And when the tears stood in her eyes after listening to my troubles, a warm feeling spread all over my body and I felt good. Something was happening inside me. What it was, I didn't know. But I began to understand: 'Fishke, you're no longer all alone in the world. You're not lone as a stone any more!' And my eyes were wet with big hot tears.

"And my wife? What a surprise! I didn't care much whether she carried on with the bastard or not. I made faces, of course, but without spirit—I didn't feel as hurt as I used to. Sometimes I even worried about what I would do if my wife suddenly said to me: 'Fishke! Enough of this wandering. Come, let's pick out a city and settle down!' I tried not to think about it, and my thoughts turned to her again—what would happen to my poor hunchback?

"But listen to this! The more I cooled toward my wife, the more she warmed up to me. More and more often she would have a good hour and be kind to me—soft as dough —and hang around my neck. But I paid for it later. She tormented me a thousand times worse than before, so that I wished I was dead. I had it from her—hot and cold. I couldn't figure out what was the matter with her. Was she crazy or just plain out of her mind? But a little later, something happened which made the blister break open. I finally understood what was eating her and what was behind her madness. It's a disgrace to talk about it."

Fishke thought for a moment. Then he scratched himself and continued his tale.

"We once arrived in some small town and, as usual, drove right to the poorhouse to set up for the night. Well, let me tell you, I've seen plenty of poorhouses in my time and know what to expect, but this one was different. Even today, whenever I think of it, I start itching all over and I have to scratch myself. This poorhouse was a very old inn, a ruin with crooked walls and a roof like a crumpled cap, turned up in front and very low in the back, almost down to the ground. This tired old poorhouse looked ready to faint. The poor building wanted to collapse and lie down to rest on the ground in a pile of dust and rubble. But the townspeople had talked it out of such nonsense. They propped it up with sticks, tied it up with string, and begged it to last for another hundred twenty years.

"What used to be a gate led into a large house. You could see daylight through the cracks in the crumbling walls. The ground was full of holes and puddles. Some of them were filled with dirty rain water that had come in through the rotten roof. Others were full of stink-

136

ing garbage that had been dumped there. Pieces of rotten straw lay all over mixed with all sorts of rags and junk: pieces of baskets, chopped-up matting, dried-out uppers of shoes, old heels and soles with rusted nails, pieces of pottery, broken barrel hoops, spokes from wheels, hair, bones, broom reeds and other trash. All this rotted on the ground and made the air so thick and stinking that you could faint.

"On the left side of the house was a greasy old door. It opened with a creak into a room with small, narrow windows that didn't set right. Most of the panes were missing; the holes were covered with fish paper, or stuffed with rags. The whole panes were very dirty and had thick layers of mold in the corners. Some were so old that they were covered with glaring yellowish-green film whose sharp reflections hurt your eyes just as scraping on glass hurts your ears. Long benches—boards lying on wooden blocks and stumps—stood along the crumbling walls and around the big stove. Wooden hooks were knocked into the walls over the benches. From the black ceiling hung several nooses with wooden rods through them. On these hooks and rods hung the greasy old coats, dresses, baskets of all the beggars who came there, some on foot, some by van. Young and old, male and female—all stayed together.

"The poorhouse was also the charity hospital. This was the place where the town's sickest beggars died. The doctor did everything he could: he cupped them, he bled them, he physicked them at the expense of *Kahal*, until their kosher souls fled from his treatment. Then the poorhouse keeper, who was also the town grave digger, buried them free.

"The poorhouse keeper and his family lived there too

in a little alcove which was an excuse for a room. Aside from being poorhouse keeper, grave digger, official in the Burial Society, inspector of the charity hospital, Queen Vashti in the *Purim* play, a bear during *Simches-Torah,* a waiter, a punster at all weddings and circumcisions, he had another business: he made wax candles. All the rich families and all the synagogues in the town bought their candles from him. And when he made a batch, there was a stink for miles around.

"When we arrived, the poorhouse keeper had more than enough guests already. He drove them along: 'You've sat here long enough. It's time to move on to some other town.' Since it was late Thursday, they had a good reason to beg for more time: 'At least until after *Shabbes!*' That night the ground, the benches, the stove were swarming with droves of people. They pushed, shoved, cursed and fought for a place to sit. It was a war between cavalry and infantry. Each tried to show the other who was stronger. During the whole uproar, a sick old man, who had been brought in the day before, was groaning in a corner. A little baby, whose foot someone had stepped on during the shoving, screamed to make you deaf.

"Later, when things quieted down a little, I found myself a corner and lay down to rest a bit. I'd hardly stretched out when I was attacked by armies of roaches, bedbugs, and fleas like bears. They wanted to eat me alive. To this day, I start itching all over when I think of that night, and I have to scratch myself. I soon saw that it's hard to fight roaches—a roach is a creature that creeps, and his partner, the bedbug, is one that stinks—and I gave up my corner to them, let them choke on it! Then I went into the front part of the house to find a place there to spend the night.

"It was very dark out there. A cold wind was blowing, howling like a pack of wolves, and whistling in through the cracks in the walls. Wisps of straw from the roof and other pieces of trash danced around like devils. Big drops of rain came in through the holes in the roof. I crawled into a corner and lay down shivering with cold. '*Ai*, my bathhouse, my bathhouse!' I groaned and moaned. 'How can I get back to my old bathhouse? It was so warm there, a real Garden of Eden, a Paradise! Oh, how happy I used to be in my Garden of Eden. I couldn't have wanted anything better, but the devil had to thrust my wife on me that I might be driven out by her to spend the rest of my years wandering over the face of the earth. That's the only thing women bring—trouble! That's all they're good for. What else can you have from them?'

"But then I remembered my hunchbacked girl and felt ashamed. She was a kind, gentle soul. It felt so good, so sunny and bright, just to sit with her and talk. Why, her little toenail was worth a thousand bathhouses! A look of hers warmed all my bones, like the sun. 'Shame on you, Fishke!' I lectured myself. 'You sin when you talk like that. Why, women make our lives sweet. A woman can make a man very happy. She can even make a heaven out of hell!'

"These sweet thoughts drove all my troubles away. I felt very good in my little corner. It wasn't cold any more. I began to read my prayers with feeling. But my eyes wouldn't stay open and I soon fell asleep. Suddenly I was awakened by a terrible scream.

" 'Just look at that creature!' someone shouted at the door and, with all his strength, threw something heavy into my part of the house. It fell to the ground like a stone with a thud. 'Look at her! Thinks she's a princess, she

XVIII

SUDDENLY FISHKE WAS SILENT. HE TURNED HIS FACE AWAY
as if he were ashamed. No matter how Alter coaxed him,
it was no use.

"*Ett* . . . Really!" Fishke muttered and blushed, reluctant to open his mouth again.

Fishke was ashamed of what he'd said, it seemed. At
first, spurred on by the heat of anger, he burst into flame
and talked like a man with a high fever. He poured out
his bitter heart in words that were far beyond his intel-
lect. These words came to him by themselves, welling up
from his soul. He forgot the world around him and talked
and talked, hardly hearing what he was saying, until,
suddenly, he awoke, somehow heard his own words, wondered at himself . . . and became embarrassed.

Who among us has not experienced, at least once in his
lifetime, a brilliant hour of inspiration, when his mouth
gave utterance to pure, true, human feelings which burst
forth like clouds of seething and steaming gases from a
fire-spouting volcano? Even upon Balaam's ass a blessed
hour descended during which he opened his mouth and
delivered a fine speech. It also happens sometimes that
even a preacher, pardon the comparison, who is forever
chewing his cud and talking nonsense enough to make
you sick, is suddenly struck with inspiration and, without
thinking, comes forth with an idea that leaves both him
and his audience gasping with wonder.

As soon as the moment of inspiration evaporates, the

ass remains an ass and the preacher, pardon the comparison, a bag of wind and . . . but that's not my point.

I used to know two men who turned the presses in a Jewish printing house. Their job consisted of turning the wheels of the press, one on each side, like two oxen; turning and turning forever, without stopping, standing in one place, day after day. Then, one day, the two of them, as though bewitched, began to crank the wheels with great ardor, full of enthusiasm. Sparks shot from their eyes and they cranked with such rapture that you might have thought they were in seventh heaven and that each turn gave birth to a thought, or an idea, which had been agitating them. A while later, when the inspiration evaporated, they looked at each other with glassy eyes in dull amazement, spat, turned their heads away, and cranked the wheels in the usual manner looking again, for all the world, like two oxen.

I glanced at Fishke, who sat speechless, and sought a means to make him talk again. Suddenly, I thought of the Golem of Reb Laib-Sarah's and how he used to rise after Red Laib said the magic word and do everything he was commanded to do. "A good idea! Welcome!" I thought. But instead of the magic words used in bygone days to waken that Golem, may he rest in peace, the magic words I was going to use to waken my Golem, may he live long, would be about the hunchbacked girl.

I fed coal to the fire and warmed him up with a conversation about his girl. In the meanwhile, I became excited myself and ended up speaking with heat:

"How many innocent children there must be who suffer because of their parents' sins! Parents who think only of themselves, who divorce each other and leave the children, their own flesh and blood, to the winds! What

"The best assignment was the one to the tax collector; the worst ones were to the synagogue and *Kahal* officials. These gentlemen took good care of themselves, but they'd hand only a few crumbs to someone else. These charity collectors always sighed about how badly off the poor folks were, but when they had one as a *Shabbes* guest, they hardly let him come close to the food. Beggars always feel that it's bad luck to have to be a guest of theirs for *Shabbes*. They avoid them like the plague. If someone is assigned to one of these officials, the other beggars laugh at him.

"The *shammes* was very angry. He shouted that there were more paupers that day than usual. 'Paupers!' he yelled. 'Why have you descended on our town like a swarm of locusts? It's impossible to take care of all of you! It's a punishment from God—a plague!' He yelled, he screamed, but the beggars pressed closer and closer. They only cared about one thing: 'Me! Give one to me!' They all shouted together. Some of them forced a few coins into the *shammes*' hand. What could the poor man do? He took the money and handed out the assignments.

"My little hunchback and I stood off to a side and watched from afar. We weren't strong enough or nervy enough to force our way in among these bears, these aristocrats of ours. Oh yes, there are aristocrats even among the poor. They're a thousand times worse than the rich. The bastard, of course, was way up front. He got two good assignments—one for himself and one for my wife. She didn't even have to bother shoving. He pointed to her, saying to the *shammes:* 'Just look at her, please. There she is—blind, the poor thing!'

"When the crowd broke up, each one with his meal ticket, my hunchback and I went up to the *shammes*, for

146

better or worse, and asked for assignments for ourselves. With a sort of sweet-sour little smile he glanced at us and didn't say a word.

" 'Take pity,' I said to him, 'on two unfortunate creatures, cripples. All week long we don't even taste a spoonful of cooked food.'

" 'There are no more assignments,' the *shammes* answered. 'You saw what just happened here. Where can I send you?'

" 'Here, take this,' I said and folded six groschen into his palm. 'It's for you. Have pity. Take care of us and it will be a *mitzvah* for you!'

" 'Look here, you . . .' The *shammes* spoke more softly. 'I don't need your money. I have one assignment left and can give it to one of you only. You can toss a coin for it if you want to.'

" 'Give it to her, to her!' I begged and pointed to my hunchback.

" 'No, no! Give it to him!' she begged, pointing to me. 'I won't take it myself.'

"We tried to talk each other into taking it. We each swore several times that under no circumstances would we take it alone. The *shammes* was moved by all this. He smoothed his beard and looked at us in a very friendly way.

" 'I'll tell you what I'll do,' he said. 'If you'll both wait at the synagogue door after the evening prayers, I'll ask for you while the people are leaving.'

"And so it was. After the evening prayers, while the congregation was leaving the synagogue, he went up to two proprietors and, pointing to us, asked them to accept us as guests for *Shabbes*. 'I really didn't have the heart to send you any guests this week,' he apologized.

147

'I almost never leave you out. But if you don't mind, please take these two paupers.'

" 'With pleasure!' they both exclaimed. 'Where is the Jew who will refuse to accept a guest for *Shabbes?* It is the one day in the week when a Jew can catch his breath. Why shouldn't he, on this holy day, take in the needy and poor and share with them God's gifts? We beg you, *Shammes!* Send us needy guests each week and don't forget us.'

"Both proprietors walked ahead followed by their sons, all neatly dressed and freshly washed. Their faces shone and they all chattered happily. It was plain that in each of them their second soul—the Jew's Sabbath soul— was in command. My little hunchback and I walked quietly behind them and felt very happy.

" 'Good *Shabbes!*' my host greeted his wife when we came into the house. She sat on a chair, neat and clean, and shone like a princess. She kissed the baby on her lap. At her side played two pretty little girls, all dressed up.

" 'God has granted me a guest for *Shabbes,* my dear, else you might not let me into the house,' he said with a smile and began to greet the members of his household with a hearty *'sholem aleichem!'* During the prayer 'Valiant Woman,' he placed himself before his wife and, still chanting the words, took the baby into his arms and kissed and petted it, while the other children joyfully gathered around him. It almost seemed as if the house were full of angels . . . I'm telling you all this because just then I thought of my little hunchback and wished she were here with me . . .

"My host was fairly well off. The Sabbath candles burned in highly polished candlesticks made of, I don't know which, real silver or Warsaw silver. The table was set with porcelain dishes and the *chalahs* were covered with a cloth napkin. A bottle of wine sparkled on the table; we each poured from it when we said *kiddush*. During the meal, the hostess served me with an open hand and begged me not to feel ashamed to eat my fill. It was wonderful. The only thing that bothered me was the thought of my poor hunchback. With each bite of fish, with each spoonful of soup and noodles, with each piece of meat, I wondered whether she was being treated as well as I.

"After the meal, they asked me to spend the night. 'Let him sleep here,' the hostess said quietly to her husband. 'Where will he go? To that stable of a poorhouse? Here, at least, he can rest for a night.'

"How I would have liked to spend the night here in this warm house in a soft bed and straighten my bones out a bit! It was just what I needed, especially after what had happened the previous night. But I thought of her. I thanked them warmly but declined to spend the night. She was having her *Shabbes* meal in a nearby house. I went there and soon we both left together.

"It was beautiful outside. The moon shone brightly and it was a pleasure to walk.

" 'Come!' I said to her. 'Let's go for a walk. There's nothing to rush back to the poorhouse for.'

"The thought of the poorhouse made a cold chill go down my back. The sick old man, who was groaning all last night, began his last fight for life in the morning and died after the evening prayer. They lay him, over the Sabbath, in that part of the house where I was going to sleep.

"We walked along and found ourselves wandering down a street of gardens and trees which filled the air with delicious odors. It was quiet all around—not a sound. Everybody had gone to bed long ago as Jews usually do after supper on Friday night. We sat down on the grass near a fence.

"For a while we just looked and didn't say a word. We were both busy with our own thoughts. Then my hunchback sighed from the depths of her heart and began to hum the sad familiar tune to herself:

> 'My father used to beat me,
> My mother used to hate me . . .

"I looked at her. Tears were rolling down her cheeks. Her face was aflame. She looked at me and smiled sadly. That look of hers took the strength out of me. My heart stopped beating and there was a pounding in my temples. I didn't know what happened to me and . . . before I knew what I was saying, the words escaped from my mouth: 'My dear soul!'

" '*Ai,* Fishke,' she said quietly, choking on her tears, 'I can't stand it much longer. How he tortures me. How he tortures me!

" 'Who?' I exclaimed in a rage. 'He? The bastard? His bones should rot!'

" '*Ai,* if you knew, Fishke. If you knew!'

"I took her hand and, with tears in my eyes, begged her to empty her bitter heart. She covered her face with both hands and bent over to me. With a trembling voice she hinted at such things, such things! That bastard should drop dead, not to arise even on Judgment Day!"

XIX

AGAIN FISHKE WAS SILENT. HE WAS SOMEHOW ANGRY AND sad at the same time. To make him talk again, I decided to tease him a little and said:

"You know, Fishke, you haven't even told us whether your hunchback is a pretty girl or not. Really, what can a hunchbacked girl have that makes her so attractive?"

"What do you mean?" Fishke asked hotly. "Since when does a Jewish girl have to be pretty? If she's pretty, she is pretty for herself and it's no one else's business. It's true, my hunchback is not bad-looking at all—she has a charming face, a beautiful head of hair, a pair of eyes like jewels —but that's none of my business! What am I, a skirt chaser, to start running after pretty girls? Nonsense! I liked her because she was good, warm, and she pitied me like a sister. In turn, I pitied her like a brother in a time of need. That's what it was!"

"Well, what's the difference?" Alter spoke up. "Pretty or not, you said that she told you something strange. What was it? *Nu, nu,* tell us!"

Alter urged him on in his fashion, Fishke started in his, I helped him out and corrected him in mine, and the story continues as follows:

"He used to pinch her, the bastard, his bones should rot! I'd noticed for a long time that he used to sidle up to my poor hunchback and pinch her. At first, I thought that he pinched her because he was a brute and enjoyed torturing and hurting other people. But, from what she told me, these were pinches of a different sort. They had a completely different taste, *tfu!* These were the pinches of sin, inspired by the devil. The bastard used to pester her. He gave her no peace. When he caught her alone, he laid it on thick with all kinds of sweet talk. He talked himself out of breath promising her mountains of gold. When he saw that promises were getting him nowhere, he began to bully her. He threatened her—he'd make her life miserable, he'd ruin her reputation, he'd throw her out in the middle of the road—and at the same time he tried to grab her by force. She usually had to tear herself out of his hands, sometimes by hitting him in the stomach and leaving him breathless. But he paid her back later with interest. He gave her the dirtiest jobs and tore pieces of flesh from her. Later on, the whole business started all over again—first sweet words, then threats. The more she avoided him, the more he followed her. When other people were present, he used to bump into her accidentally and pinch her, just so, for no reason at all.

"Ugly scenes like these took place quite often, but what happened the day before was terrible! *Feh!* I shouldn't even repeat it! After the uproar in the poorhouse, when the whole crowd was asleep and my poor hunchback slept doubled up near the door, she was suddenly awakened by someone whispering in her ear. It was the bastard!

" 'You must be very uncomfortable here, you poor girl,' he said to her with pity. 'Come, I have a good spot for you. You'll be able to get a good rest.'

"She thanked him for being so kind, and told him she was comfortable enough where she was. He began insisting that she should come with him. He told her that he knew all about her and me. He threatened that he would make her life miserable and grind me into the dust. The devil take him, the bastard! He could act like a wolf and an innocent lamb both rolled into one! Again he tried sweet words and threats but he became too bold. She smacked his cheek so that his teeth rattled. He flew into a rage, picked her up like a murderer and flung her out of the door. What happened after that, you already know.

"After my poor hunchback told me this, I sat glumly for a long while. A worm was gnawing away at me. The mere thought of the bastard made me burn with anger. At the same time, I had a warm feeling of pity for her and another feeling, too. I don't know what to call it, but it drew me to her—it made my heart pound. Suddenly, it beat so hard I thought I'd faint. I took her hand, which still covered her face, and spoke to her with a voice that was not my own.

" 'My darling! I'd give my life for your sake!'

" 'Oh, Fishke!' she sighed, moving closer to me and resting her head on my shoulder.

"The whole world seemed so rosy then. My body felt wonderfully warm and light. I comforted her and spoke to her like to a dear sister. I cheered her and told her not to worry: 'With God's help all will be well.' I swore I would be like a brother to her forever. She gazed into my eyes and smiled sweetly. Then she lowered her eyes and said:

" 'I don't know why it is, Fishke, but I feel so good now! I really want to live.'

"We talked for a while lightheartedly about how, with God's help, the future would be kind to us both and grant all our wishes.

"Suddenly we heard a tapping not far from us. I got up and walked in the shadow of the fence. On the other side of the alley, a man was fumbling with a cellar door. Something urged me, drove me forward a few more paces. I looked closely and . . . aha! His bones should rot, it was the bastard! He finally forced the lock open and disappeared into the cellar. He probably wanted to steal the things that were stored there for the Sabbath. Like a lightning flash, the thought struck me: 'Fishke! This is your chance to avenge your poor hunchback. Now, while there is time, lock the cellar door and let him lie there like a bear in a trap! Tomorrow they'll find him and he'll get his proper reward!'

"For the first time, I knew the sweet taste of revenge! How good, how delicious it was! My blood was on fire in my veins. I was drunk with power! It took only a minute to dash up to the door and slam it shut. 'Lie there, you dog!' I laughed to myself. I seized the hasp and tried to force it over the staple, but it was bent! I pulled, but it was no use! It wouldn't give. I grasped it with both hands and took a deep breath for a last try. I was just about to force it on when a strong tug from inside pulled the door open and I flew into the cellar, banging into the bastard on the threshold.

" 'So, Reb Fish!' said the bastard after we had stared at each other in silence for a moment. 'It is on my account that you were puttering with the cellar door and violating the Sabbath! I surely appreciate it. Come, my kitten. Since you're visiting, come, let me entertain you. . . .' He shoved me down the stairs. I almost broke my neck and stretched out flat on the ground. 'And now, my dear guest, take this as an advance!' And he gave me a resounding blow in the back. 'And you won't mind waiting here until I fetch the roast chicken and the plate of fish that I was going to leave behind because you frightened me when you were fooling with the door.' He struck me again.

" 'Count, Fishke!' he exclaimed. 'Here's one, and two, and three, four, five . . . that's to settle my account. And now for the hunchback's! Count, Fishke! Here's nine, and ten! Aren't you ashamed to be dragging around at night with a girl in secret places? Here's twelve, and thirteen! I saw you before, ah yes I did, prowling around the back alleys with her. There's sixteen, if I'm not mistaken, and seventeen!'

"My blood boiled up at his last words.

" 'You bastard!' I shouted. 'Don't you dare to mention her name!' I jumped up swiftly and sank my teeth into him. It was quite a fight; I with my teeth and he with his hands. He tore me away with brute force. Then he held me with both hands and squeezed. It was terrible! Then he threw me away like a ball.

"Thank your lucky star that you're getting off so easy. I don't feel like continuing this conversation with you. Stay here, Fishke, and rest up for tomorrow. Instead of *gefillte* fish they'll have a live fish tomorrow. Good night! Any message for your wife? I'll give her your regards as soon as I get back.'

"With these words, he shut the door and left.

"When I came to, the first thing I did was run to the door and try it. I tugged and pulled, but it was no use! He had locked it well from outside. I didn't know what to do next. I was afraid to make any noise because the owners might hear me. But to stay here was also dangerous. I was dizzy with fear, with anger and with aches from the bastard's blows. I went back down the stairs and threw myself down on the ground. But the thought of what would happen when they found me here tomorrow, of how they would hang out the welcome sign for me, of how the

whole town would come running to see the thief—these thoughts tortured me and didn't let me rest. Everyone who believed in God would beat me and no excuse would be good enough. While I was imagining these things, I thought I felt something crawling over me. I put out my hand and grabbed a rat which quickly slid through my fingers with a squeal. I jumped up in terror. I felt nauseous and broke out in a cold sweat.

"In the darkness, I groped around—I could hardly stand on my feet—until I felt a cold, damp wall. I leaned against it and thought bitterly: 'Lord of Nations, what kind of life is this? Why do you punish me like this? Wouldn't it have been better, for me and for the world, if I'd never been born? Why do I always . . . always have to be despised?' This last thought broke my heart and I burst into tears. 'Oh, God, where are you?'

"I stood there like a statue without moving. What would happen to me? Suddenly, the door creaked and a thin band of light cut the darkness before my eyes. I could hear soft steps coming down the stairs. My hair stood on end from fright. Here, right now, they would seize me and punish me like a thief. I stood there with hanging head and knocking knees, when I heard someone call my name cautiously: 'Fishke, Fishke!' And, in a moment, I saw her at my side—my hunchback. I came to life and shouted for joy.

" 'Sha,' she whispered and took my hand. 'Come quickly, let's get out of here.'

" 'My darling! You saved my life!' I shouted, forgetting the danger, I was so confused. For the first time, I must confess, I kissed her there in the cellar.

"I asked her how she came here, but she reminded me that we were in someone's cellar at night. 'Come quickly.

I'll tell you everything later,' she said and led me out into the street. While we were walking along, she told me what had happened.

"A few minutes after I was gone, she had a feeling that something was wrong, that she ought to go and see where I was. She walked to the end of the fence, looked around, and saw someone on the other side of the street bending over a door and fumbling with the lock. Thinking it was me, she decided to go across. But when she came close, she heard these words: 'And now, Reb Fish! You can lie there and rot like a dog. I've locked it carefully, never fear!' Before she had time to get over her fright, the bastard stood before her. He pinched her and snickered, 'Good *Shabbes*, it's the *rebitsin* herself! What a girl! Drags around in the middle of the night and makes pious faces! Humph! Get home, you slut!' And shoving her along with his knee, he forced her to go his way. All the way back, he kept on looking around and shifting the loaded basket from one shoulder to the other. At the same time, he didn't forget for a minute to use sweet words and threats on her. She went along glumly. She knew I was in trouble and there was no way for her to help me because the bastard made her stay within reach.

"Suddenly, a company of Jews appeared on their way from a *Ben Zochor*. They were happy and talked and laughed at the top of their lungs as is the custom among the children of Israel. The bastard hopped to a side quickly and ran down a narrow alley. My hunchback also jumped aside and ran the other way.

"Her first thought was to get back and help me. But, imagine her anguish when she got lost in the crooked alleys and side streets. She knew I was in great danger, that she had to get to me as soon as possible, that every mo-

158

ment was precious. And here she was, lost and unable to find her way back. She wandered around for a good while until, with God's help, she found the cellar and set me free.

"We walked along and talked happily. I to her: 'My darling! You stood by me in a time of need.' And she to me: 'Fishke! Yesterday, you were like a brother to me. Remember? Back there in the poorhouse?' But when we came close to the poorhouse, we both fell under a spell of gloom and our tongues froze. Our hearts told us that we could expect only trouble and that this night would not pass smoothly.

"Half of the gate to the poorhouse was closed. The other half was partly open so that part of the house was lit up by the street lamp. When we came up to the door, we both stopped with dread in our hearts. I went in first. The first thing I saw when I poked my head through the door was the bastard sitting with my wife. The two of them were stuffing themselves with the food he had stolen. The bastard whispered into her ear and soon disappeared. She got up in a rage and fell upon me, screaming:

" 'You so-and-so! The devil take your father's father! Do you think you can drag around all night with that slut of yours, that harlot? Do you think I don't know what you're up to? I've known all about it for a long time. I've been choking it down in my poor heart. Is this the thanks I get for my kindness, for taking you into the world among people, for making a somebody out of you? Do you think, you cur of curs, that you'll get away with it? Oh, no! I'll show you, the devil take your father's father, and your slut, the devil take her father's mother and her mother's father! I'll show you both. You'll learn not to fool with me. Here, take that, and that!' And she began to beat me. 'Here's for today and there's for yesterday and there's for before. There, there, there—may you drop dead!'

"I barely managed to get out of her clutches alive and ran out into the street. She stood outside for a while, shouting and screaming. Then she went back in again, screaming, 'Lie out there like a dog!' She slammed the door shut and locked it.

"My poor hunchback and I stood outside and looked at each other. We both felt miserable. Our hearts were heavy from this latest misfortune. Our troubles wouldn't let us stand idle very long. We started off and followed our noses. We walked along in silence, each thinking his own thoughts. When I finally looked up, I saw that we had wandered into the yard of the synagogue. My heart wept when I saw how tired my hunchback looked. This was her second night without rest. Where could we find a place to spend the night? Just then, I got an idea—the women's gallery in the synagogue!

"With God's help, we managed to get to the top of the rickety stairs which swung and swayed beneath our feet. We pushed open the door at the head of the stairs and tripped on something warm and soft in the dark. Suddenly, something was running and hopping all around us, on top of us, and over us in the darkness. We were hit in front, in back, in the sides—we couldn't tell where we would be hit next. I thrashed about wildly and finally seized a beard! What do you think it was? It was the beard of a goat! The town goats, as is the custom, had been sleeping in the women's gallery with the billy goat!

" 'Where are you?' I called my hunchback. 'Don't be afraid. The place is full of goats, may the Evil Eye not harm them! A town with this many goats can't be poor!'

I rounded up the goats and herded them out the door. They would have to swallow their pride and spend this night outside. I said good night to my hunchback and soon left myself, closing the door behind me.

"When I got down to the last step, the billy goat was waiting for me with his head and long horns lowered. He was in a rage because I had insulted his wives by chasing them out. I wrestled with him for a while, but I couldn't get rid of him. He dodged my kicks. Finally, I managed to slip inside the door to the men's synagogue.

"There, on the tables and benches, Cabbalists lay stretched out like princes and whistled to each other through their noses in all the tones of the scale. It was a pleasure to see, may the Evil Eye not harm them, how soundly they slept. Cabbalists really have it soft in the world, I thought, and in my heart I envied them. They are an altogether different type of beggar—somehow they're respectable. I found a place for myself near the stove, threw myself on a bench and fell soundly asleep. But it was not my lot to have any pleasure in life at all. It seemed like only a few minutes later that someone shook me, saying: 'Get up, young man! Up, up, please!'

"I rubbed my eyes and saw a group of Jews looking at me very seriously. This was the Society of Psalm Sayers. It was their custom to come to the synagogue early on *Shabbes* morning to recite the psalms. There was nothing else for me to do. I had to get up. I washed my hands and sat down, barely able to keep my eyes open. I yawned, stretched and recited the psalms together with them.

women in my market place too. *"Sholem aleichem,* all of
you!" I said, as if to myself. "God knows, I'd be only too
glad never to see your faces or hear your names again.
That's how sick you make me now. But what can I do?
Since the devil himself has brought you to life again, I
can't just ignore you, but being something of a writer, I'll
have to please him and say a word about each of you!"

"Wait a bit, Fishke! If you please, Reb Alter!" I exclaimed. "There's something I have to tell you, but I have
to think about it a little." And while I was thinking about
it, I winked at one of my characters from a charity society.
"Come on, now! Up on the stage with you!" He twisted
and turned, kicked his legs, like a bound rooster to be
sacrificed on *Yom Kippur.* The other characters looked at
me angrily, motioning me to keep quiet. "Fools!" I
thought to myself. "I'll pay no more attention to you than
to last year's snow. You won't frighten me by putting a
bearskin on your head and crying, 'Boo!' You're mon-
keys, not bears . . ." The devil in me became excited
and urged me on: "That's it, that's the way! Get them up
on the witness stand, one and all of them, those fine gentlemen!"

"Listen, please, Reb Alter! It's quite a story. In a Jewish town, the wealthier gentlemen, as their custom was,
decided to . . ." Thus I began to tell my tale and stopped
in the middle of a sentence as if the words were choking
me. The women winked at me beseechingly: "Good,
sweet, dear Reb Mendele! Have mercy, don't tell the tale!"
Their feminine charm made me soft as dough. Each sweet
glance from their burning eyes made me softer until I almost melted altogether. And then I remembered my vow
to buy my way into the Society of Good Uncles. "The
devil take the lot of you!" I said to myself with a smile,

and, turning to Alter, I continued: "They, I mean those fine gentlemen in that town . . . Somehow, I don't feel like telling that story today. They can all go to the devil. I hope you won't mind, Reb Alter!"

"On the contrary! I'm in full agreement. For my part, too, they can all go to the devil. But, what kind of manners is it to interrupt someone, to break into his story, and tell your own?" Thus spoke Alter, and glared at me a while, shrugging his shoulders as if to say: "The man's like a sieve. Words pour from him like water! Who needs his stories? What good are they, can you tell me?" And, waving his hand hopelessly, he turned to Fishke and said: "*Nu,* what's next? Let's get to the point."

Fishke began in his fashion, I helped him along in mine, and Alter urged him on in his fashion, and the story continues as follows:

"Time passed and my wife and I drifted further and further apart. She became even more attached to the bastard; they were a real pair of pals by now. They went begging together, like a prince and a princess, from house to house. It didn't make any difference to me any more. My head was troubled by my poor hunchback. She never left my mind for a minute. 'Go ahead, both of you,' I said to myself. 'For my part the two of you can go to hell!' When I met the pair of them by accident, the bastard sneered at me, as if to say: 'Well, I sure fixed your wagon, didn't I?' I usually spat and went my way, thinking: 'And even if you do drag around with her from house to house, what's the good of it to you? She is a married woman, heh-heh! She's nailed down. I've fixed your wagon too, haven't I? Eat your heart out.'

"I was now begging from house to house with a little old man, one of the bastard's bunch, as mean as they come, and just as crooked as the bastard himself. He made good use of me; everybody gave him alms. He walked in with such a piteous look, heaved such a sad sigh from the depths of his heart when he pointed to me, that you would have sworn that here was a heartbroken father with his crippled child.

" 'Limp, Fishke! Limp well, my boy!' he would say and poke me from behind when we entered a house. 'Make faces, and sigh! Sigh, you dog! They pay me well for every one of your sighs.'

"On our way, he used to teach me how to act my part better. He cursed the rich, pinched and poked me, and called me names—'The devil take you!' or 'Drop dead!' —all with a smile or a grin. Once, for a joke, he gave me such a blow in my chest, right here under my heart, that I almost passed out. He kept the money. It was hard for me to tear even a groschen out of him. 'What do you need money for, Fishke?' he used to tease. 'You're a treasure yourself. May your limping get worse and may you look sicker and sicker until you bite the dust, my fine fellow!'

"Once I demanded my share hotly and refused to take no for an answer. Necessity forced me to this. When he saw that I wouldn't give up so easily, he unleashed his nasty tongue: 'Shut your mouth, you lame dog! Do you think you're going to ride for nothing in my wagon? Do you think I'm going to carry a piece of carrion like you around for free? You worm! I'll tell your wife about this. I don't know you and I don't have to argue with you. I know only your wife! She gave you to me. It's from her that I got a piece of goods like you and it's with her that I'll settle my accounts.'

"Things were bad. I saw now that I was to the band what a bear is to a gypsy. They led me around by the nose and made money from me. They took my wife from me. They tricked her and now she was helping them against me. She handed me over to this band of thieves and robbers like a piece of goods for sale! Things were really bitter!

"I also saw that it was all over between my wife and me. We'd never live together again. Then why, I asked myself, should I stay here? I should run away right now, if I could. To spend an extra day with these thieves was a sin in the eyes of God. After all, these people had no God. They wouldn't dip their finger into cold water, if it meant work! They had thrown off their yoke. They wouldn't touch anything resembling honest work. They only sponged on others and sucked Jewish blood. Why, they were the blood enemies of all other Jews!

"Then I took a close look at myself: the time I had spent with this pack of wicked people left its mark on me. I wasn't the same as before. Many of their nasty ways had rubbed off on me. The best way to be rid of all the pain and wickedness was to tear myself away from them and avoid them like the plague. But what about her? How could I leave her, my poor hunchback, with them? I felt as though I stood on the edge of a deep pit—dark and black, like hell itself. In one ear, a voice cried: 'Don't gamble with your soul, Fishke! For God's sake, run away!' In the other ear, I heard my hunchback calling: 'Fishke, Fishke!'

"I had to choose one or the other: either the bright world, away from sin, pain and evil—or this hell, but together with her. I cried my eyes out and, may God forgive my sins, I stayed with the band of thieves.

"Later on I got the idea of running away together with my hunchback. But there was no point to this unless I

167

could first get a divorce from my wife. After all, what would be the sense in my wandering around with an unmarried girl? Everyone would wonder and think ugly thoughts about us. There was only one remedy—a divorce! But would my wife give me a divorce? If I asked for one she would refuse just for spite! Her greatest pleasure lately was to hurt me and do me dirt. But I wasn't going to be frightened off. I decided to get what I wanted by hook or crook. Maybe God would have mercy. In the meanwhile, I kept my secret to myself and didn't breathe a word about it to anyone.

"Ever since my argument with the old man, I refused to beg with anyone from the band. This caused me all sorts of trouble. But I stuck to it. If it was the last thing I ever did, I would not be a bear for these gypsies any more. The bastard and his pack were very angry about this and showed me how they felt, with their hands and fists, whenever they could. While they were beating me once, they cried: 'Why should we let you ride along for nothing, you useless garbage, if you refuse to work, if you refuse to earn anything? Get out and go to hell!'

"This very minute!' I answered. 'But first give me back my wife!'

"They looked at each other and broke into loud laughter. Of course, when I said, 'Give me back my wife!' that was only an excuse. What I really meant was: 'Keep her, keep your bargain and make her give me a divorce.' I ached all over from the beatings they gave me for my stubbornness, but at least I had the pleasure of thinking: 'This will help me get what I'm after. They'll see that I am stubborn and useless to them. They'll want to get rid of me and this will be useful in getting my divorce.'

XXI

" 'BASSIA!' I ONCE CALLED TO MY WIFE AND WENT UP TO
her gently. We were alone. I thought I'd try to get what
I was after through kindness. I wanted to sound her out
about a divorce. 'Bassia, what do you have against me?'

" 'Drop dead, Fishke!' she said.

" 'There you go again!' I grumbled as if in anger. 'I
talk gently to her. I try to please her, but she tells me to
drop dead! Why?'

" 'Then, have a stroke!' she said, her face twisted with
anger, and moved away.

" 'May you live long, Bassia!' I answered gently. 'Forget
this foolishness and let's live together as God has commanded.'

" 'Drop dead, Fishke my dear, together with your harlot!'

" 'A-a-a-h! Better you should drop dead together with
your bastard!' I said to myself. But aloud I said: 'Listen
to me, Bassia! If you don't want to live a decent life together, there's a simple way out, that's why Jews have a
divorce. Once and for all, red or dead!'

" 'Aha, he's hankering after his harlot! He wants to get
rid of his wife and hop-skip after that hussy! You'll never
live to see the day! You'll sooner bite the dust! She won't
get it so easily, that slut of yours. She'll plow the ground
with her nose for me first. Do you hear me, Fishele? The
devil take your father's fathers!'

"And my wife let loose with such wild cries that I showed her a clean pair of heels and was gone.

"I saw no way out. Things were bad any way I looked at them. I didn't have it easy myself—the band really gave it to me. But they rode all over my poor hunchback. My wife treated her like a servant. If she didn't like something, she took it out on the poor girl. The bastard, of course, tortured her in his own way. Our lives were pitiful. The only time we could catch our breaths in peace was late at night, when everybody else was asleep. Then we both stole away for a few minutes to talk and pour our bitter hearts out to each other.

"One night we were both sitting together near the Big Synagogue. The sky was covered with stars. There wasn't a living soul in sight. She sat hunched over on a stone near me and wept. With tears streaming down her cheeks, she sadly hummed the familiar words of her song:

'My father used to beat me,
'My mother used to hate me . . .'

"Each word cut into my heart like a knife. I tried to cheer her, I tried to give her hope: 'It won't be long, God willing, and we'll be free.' I wanted to make her see how we would live later, after we'd be released from our torment, with the help of the One Above. I tried to make each detail stand out like it really would be. I told her about the stone bathhouse of Glupsk with its cracks and crannies. I would get to be watchman after a while. She might also be able to find some work there. Maybe she could do mending or darning. And if this didn't work out, there were all sorts of other ways to make a living in Glupsk. For beggars, Glupsk is the Promised Land. The city is big, and the houses are many, like dust in a heap.

The people there are plain folk, with no fancy ceremonies. They all do as they please and nobody cares. For example, well-to-do merchants walk around in rags, dirty and unwashed, and—nothing! Or they go strolling in bright daylight in greasy coats, unbuttoned, with coattails flying, and —nothing! Or, on the other hand, you'll sometimes see beggars in velvets or silks and, again—nothing! in short, in Glupsk it's hard to tell the beggars apart from the rich, either by their dress or their actions. It often happens that the men who collect money for charity are beggars themselves, and together with the rich make a nice living from the contributions. One hand washes the other and it's a good life. It's no shame to be poor. With a little luck, a man can do very well for himself. There are many men who only a short time ago were unknown, low-down lackeys or beggars and now they're the bigwigs, the leaders, the wheels of the town! 'Even I, as you see me sitting here, can become a somebody, a director or a manager of some sort, and God willing, things will be good. We will live in riches and honor. Don't laugh, dear soul! I'm not out of my mind. Things like that happen often in Glupsk; you just have to believe in God and in yourself. And you must be a good Jew . . . with humility. *Ach,* Glupsk, Glupsk! How long will it be before I can tear myself free from this dirty pack of thieves and fly back to you, Mother!'

" '*Oy,* Fishke! I don't have the strength to stand it much longer,' my hunchback said, sighing from the depths of her heart. She rested her head on my shoulder while her face pleaded for mercy. I smoothed her hair, cheered her and tried to give her hope. She became happier, looked straight into my eyes and laughed.

" 'Fishke,' she said softly, 'you're the only one I have

in the whole world. You're my father, my brother, my friend, everything! Fishke, be faithful to me and don't forget me. Swear it here, at the synagogue, where the risen dead are praying now—my father may even be among them, my father whom I hardly knew. He is my witness. Swear to me that you'll always be faithful.'

"I started working for a divorce in real earnest. I argued with my wife until I was blue in the face. Finally, we made an agreement:

"I would turn over to her the little money I had saved during the time I had been working by myself. I would also play the bear for the band for all of the coming winter. They could take me from house to house and all the alms they collected would go to my wife. This would be her payment for the return of the marriage contract. When the bastard heard this, he smiled and beat me to within an inch of my life. Then he congratulated me on my wisdom. Once more, I played the bear. Again I was a valued piece of goods. Again, I went from house to house with the little old man. I had to limp, sigh, make faces and play the game as he directed.

"After Passover we stopped in a little town in the province of Kherson. At first, I kept on working according to my promise. But one day I declared: 'Enough! I've done my share.' My wife was surprised and wanted a few days to think it over. Finally, she replied: 'Fine! Tomorrow we'll be divorced.'

"I couldn't sit still or stand in one place, I was so happy! I felt like being out in the fresh air. I walked the streets for a long time. I even begged with spirit, thinking to myself that it wouldn't hurt me to have a few spare groschens at hand now that I was leaving the band. My begging went very well—it was a long time since I'd had such a good day. Money poured in hand over fist. When God wants to help a man, He takes care of everything! Wherever I walked in, I did not leave emptyhanded. I was even lucky enough to walk into a house where a briss was taking place. The guests had all had a few drinks and were happy and generous. I was given a whole kiddush-glass full of brandy, a big piece of sponge cake, money, and a roll shaped like a rose.

"I controlled myself and didn't even touch a crumb. I hid all the good things deep in my bosom so as to have a present for my hunchback when I came back. You should have seen how happy I was on the way back, thinking all along:

" 'Tonight, when the whole band is asleep, I'll give her the goodies. Let her have some pleasure too, poor thing. She is so miserable, so wretched. In her whole life she has never had a sweet moment. Now she'll know that Fishke is her brother and guards her like the apple of his eye. He won't even eat unless he can share the best things with her.'

"I pictured the two of us sitting near the Big Synagogue and enjoying ourselves. She was eating the cake with great pleasure. I was saying to her: 'My dear soul! May it do you good! May it be a good sign. God grant that we shall soon eat sponge cake to celebrate our own happiness!' And then I told her the good news: that tomorrow I would be free; my wife was giving me a divorce. And she, my poor dear, shone and beamed like the sun. The two of us planned how we'd run away from the band of thieves unseen and be free again. With God's help, all would be well.

"With these thoughts I walked back, dreaming about my happy future. I even saw a water carrier with full

173

ish children be protected from it!" We also used to laugh at someone in love just as we laughed at the village idiot. But, I also remember that whenever this disease struck, it was either among the very wealthy or the very poor. The respectable folks in between were immune, they never caught it.

I often used to think that there was something remarkable in this. What did it all mean? The stories of old peasant women with their love potions and herbs—those were all nonsense—I was never satisfied with them. Many folks considered me somewhat of a heretic because of this. That was just as bad as not believing in witchcraft, in evil spirits, or in the *Tatar,* who can cure all ills with his magic powders! I long sought a better explanation and, at last, I thought I found one.

The very wealthy have it very good in this world. They have everything: food, the best of drink, the most expensive things, all with no worries and no headaches. Really, what do they lack except, maybe, a good fever? Having nothing better to do they play lovey-dovey. Do they do so in earnest or just for entertainment? That's their secret. On the other hand, the beggars also have it good in their own way. Aside from a good fever, they have nothing to lose. They have no headaches or worries either, since they sponge on the rest of the people. So they, too, can afford to take up such nonsense. Love affairs and marriages for love are customary only among the upper and lower classes. The rest of us, folks of a middling sort, have our minds in a bowl of *borsch!* We're too busy earning our daily bread, trying to make a living. Our first worry is business. Everything is business; even marriage is a business. We procure a wife for ourselves: first, we haggle over the price, over the dowry, over each and every little

176

detail to our heart's content. All this is carefully written into the engagement contract. Even the fur cap or the sabbath capote which goes into the dowry is listed in the contract. When all conditions are properly fulfilled, as stated in writing, "Then come, dear bride, let's go under the *chupeh* together with the matchmaker, the master of ceremonies, and the whole pack of synagogue officials who all expect some commission. Be a wife, bear children, suffer and get wrinkled and gray together with me until we both reach one hundred and twenty; that is, if you can stand living that long and don't wish to die before your time. Whether you are pretty or ugly, clever or stupid, that's your affair—it's all the same to me, for a wife is a wife. We are not lords or noblemen. We have no time to pay attention to such foolishness. We are Jews, merchants, traders, storekeepers, busy with our business."

There's many a Jew in my class who hardly ever talks to his wife, never eats at the same table with her, rarely looks at her, and thinks that this is as it should be. Husband and wife are both pleased with this arrangement and, should the subject come up, they wish such a life for all good people and for their children, too. When the wife dies, the man sits in mourning like a good Jew for the prescribed seven days and soon procures himself a second wife, sometimes even before the prescribed thirty-day waiting period has run out. And, in the same way, his third, fourth and fifth wife is procured, and so on until the last old woman whom he marries in his old age, usually under the pretext that he will go to Jerusalem with her to die.

Among Jews, this whole procedure goes under the name of fulfilling a *mitzvah*, of doing God's bidding. The same holds true when Jews speak of the way they eat on *Shab-*

177

"For the first few days there, I was more dead than alive. I roamed around all alone, a stranger in the big city, and didn't know what to do with myself. Everything was new to me, new and strange. I couldn't find a poorhouse like in other Jewish towns. There were no houses to go into either. In our Jewish cities, there are houses—plain houses, nothing fancy, one-story, with the entrance off the street. Push the door, just crack it open, and you're smack in the middle of the house. No big ceremonies, everything you need is right there. Do you want to eat or sleep? Do you need water? Here it is. The pail of slops? Right there. Go ahead, wash your hands to your heart's content, but say your prayers first. Why, here are the people who live here—man, wife and children! Say: 'Help a poor man, in the name of the Lord!' Put out your hand and you'll get something. Kiss the *Mezuzah* on the way out, and go your way in peace. Also, in our cities, it's easy to tell a Jewish house from the outside. There's a little pile of garbage, a little puddle of dirty water, and the windows, the walls, the roof all shout together: 'This is a Jewish house!' The smell alone tells you that a Jew lives here. . . .

"But in Odessa, the houses are crazy. They're so high! First, you go through a gate into a courtyard. From there you have to climb stairs and look for doors. When you finally find one, it's locked! There's a bell, a knocker, or some other trick. You stand there with a heavy heart. You realize how poor you are, how low you are, that you're a man without a face. Then you work up courage and respectfully ring the bell, just a little ring, almost nothing at all, as if you're ashamed of it. You feel as though you have said a dirty word or sent his father's father's father to the devil, and you run away before the door opens.

. . . Sometimes the door opens before you can run away and you're at the mercy of an angry cook or butler, or it turns out that a non-Jew lives there! 'How can that be?' you wonder. 'What kind of city is this? And what kind of houses are these? Where are all the beggars with their baskets?'

"I roamed the streets and looked around carefully. I was hoping I would meet another beggar with his basket from whom I could find out the right way to beg here. But, as if for spite, I saw no beggars. As I wandered this way, I saw a young man in the distance, dressed like a German, walking like a man who isn't sure of his way. He looked at all the houses and crossed from one side of the street to the other. 'This fellow,' I said to myself, 'must be a stranger here. I'll follow him and see what he does.' He went into a yard, I right behind him. He went up a flight of stairs, I—also up. He knocked on a door and went into a foyer. I waited just outside the door. Soon a man appeared, with a shaven face. It must have been the owner himself. The young man gave him some sort of book which he pulled out of his pocket, a pocket as broad and deep as a basket! The shaven one looked at the title page and flung the book back at the young man with an angry shout: 'Leave me in peace! What do I need your junk for?' The young man pleaded with him, praised himself to the sky, claiming that he had a real jewel here. But it was no use and the poor fellow went out shamefaced and heartbroken. I went in and simply begged for alms. They gave me a few groschen and I ran out with a joyful heart. 'Now,' I thought, 'I've found the right way. God sends flax to the spinner, beer to the inn-keeper, and a stranger to the beggar as a guide. I must not lose sight of this fellow!' He did very badly. In one place he was told, 'Go your way, young man! We don't need your wares!' In another, the door was simply slammed in his face. He left empty-handed and angry every time. I wasn't doing badly at all, may the Evil Eye not harm me. I took a groschen or two or three each time —whatever they gave me.

" 'What's going on?' I wondered. 'What kind of a beggar is this? I never heard of anything like this in my whole life. It must be a custom here—beggars with books! Newfangled beggars, and they're dressed like Germans. What fools! Why beg with books and get a fig for your troubles when you can simply beg for alms and get something! I like our grandfathers' customs better: you go from house to house simply, without tricks. That way I can do better than others with their books. Whatever he was, fool or no, I kept close behind my beggar with the books. I trailed after him and was careful to keep him from seeing me. At first, he didn't, but later he must have felt that someone was dragging after him and he was very annoyed. He began to stop and look around often, seeking a way to get rid of me. I looked the other way, as if I didn't even know he was there, and followed after him. In my heart, I thought, 'Oh, no! You won't get away from me, brother o'mine! Although you don't do anyone any good, especially yourself, still, I need you. You are like a guiding star to me, sage o'mine!'

"Finally, we got into a scrape in one apartment. The owner had just sat down to eat when my beggar walked in. They had a big argument. My beggar tried to sell. One word led to another and the owner became very angry. He showed him the door and finding me there, sent us both off to the devil together. Our common lot naturally led us to get to know each other better. As we started

182

down the stairs, my partner looked at me angrily. I turned my eyes away and didn't know what to do. I waited for him to go first. We stood there like that for a few minutes and both felt bad. Then my partner said to me:

"'Just what do you want, Mister?'

"'Me? Nothing!' I answered. 'The same as you.'

"'The same as I?' asked my partner, looking me up and down from head to toe with great wonder. 'Are you also an author?'

"I didn't know what 'author' meant. I thought it was the German word for what we, in plain Yiddish, call 'beggar.' So I answered him in his own language:

"'Yes, an author.'

"'And what have you done?'

"'Oh, I've done quite well,' I answered, thinking to myself that I had done a sight better than he had. 'About forty groschen.'

"'And what's the name of your opus?' he asked.

"'He's talking German to me again,' I thought. What he meant to say was: 'And what's your name, partner?'

"'Fishke!' I answered to the point.

"'May I have the honor of becoming acquainted with *Fishke?*' he asked with a sugary smile.

"'*Ach!* By all means! It's my pleasure, upon my word,' I answered warmly, and gave him a big grin.

"'Well? Where is this opus?'

"'Why, here I am standing right before you, may you prosper!'

"'Go to hell!' he exploded and ran off in a rage.

"When I came out of the yard, I saw my partner running like a madman. He was already halfway down the street. Then he ducked into a side alley and vanished. I stood there as though I had been slapped and wondered

183

what was the matter with him. He must have gone mad! One minute he was nice and friendly and the next minute he is in a rage. What did I say to him? I even answered him with his own German words—'author' and 'opus'! In plain Yiddish, all they mean is 'beggar' and 'basket'! For my part, he could go to the devil, too!

XXIII

"IT WASN'T LONG BEFORE I WAS MORE FAMILIAR WITH Odessa. I got to know all its side streets and alleys. I had figured the city out and now knew where to open doors. Odessa is like one of those tricky little snuff boxes—you have to find the catch. Once you know that it opens easily, you can stick your fingers in and take a pinch whenever you want to. I discovered a whole new world of houses, the kind I needed, just like back home in Glupsk. I found all the beggars I wanted! Armies of them, and of all different kinds—beggars with baskets and beggars without baskets—types you could find only in Odessa and nowhere else. There were Jerusalem Jews and Frankish, Turkish and Persian Jews who babbled away in the Holy Tongue; there were old paupers with their wives, and also without their wives, who claimed they were on their way to Jerusalem to die, but, in the meanwhile, stayed on in Odessa, had more children, and thought the world owed them a living; there were wives whose husbands had deserted them; there were women with spasms and men with fits who came here for a cure on the coast; there were Cabbalists of the old homey sort who used to loaf in the Houses of Study; then there were the new-fangled Cabbalists with shaven faces who used to loaf in the cafés and taverns together with the Galicians and Frenchmen; there were refined beggars without a groschen to their name who dressed like rich men; and there were others who

185

even owned their own houses but dressed in rags and tatters like the poorest of the poor.

"The beggars that I met there from Glupsk all praised Odessa to the sky, but I could never see in what way they were better off. One of them explained to me that the difference between a beggar in Glupsk and in Odessa was this: in Glupsk, a beggar eats his dry crust of bread in dreariness and weariness; in Odessa, he eats the same dry crust of bread to the accompaniment of a hurdy-gurdy. There's a hurdy-gurdy in the street, in the houses, in the taverns, in the theaters. Even in the synagogue—forgive the comparison, *feh!*—there's a hurdy-gurdy. There is always excitement in Odessa; something is always happening! The air whistles and screeches. Walk by a tavern, and there's always a drunkard at the open door, groaning and singing 'Pretty Maiden'—that's a song of theirs there. Across the table from him, happy, tipsy Jews sing psalms and prayers to merry marching tunes!

"One day I was walking at the side of the street when I felt a sharp blow in my back. I decided not to make a fuss, thinking that someone in the crowd had accidentally bumped into me. But soon I felt another blow, like with a piece of wood. I turned around—and there was Yontl, the cholera groom from Glupsk, sitting on the street on a little wooden platform with wheels and two wooden pushers, one in each hand! He leaned on one pusher and held the other one up in the air with a grin. He was glad that he had run into me. I was also very glad to find Yontl. He and I used to be good friends in Glupsk. I was at his wedding on the cemetery during the cholera epidemic, may we be saved from such a calamity today!

" 'Well, Fishke!' he greeted me. 'So you're here in our Odessa too? Quite a city, my Odessa, isn't she!'

186

"Seeing that I shrugged my shoulders and wasn't impressed, he looked offended, as though I'd insulted his dignity.

" 'You think your Glupsk is a city? A worm in a sour apple has no idea that there are sweet ones! Wait, I'll show you my Odessa, then we'll hear what you say!'

"Yontl told me how well liked he was in Odessa. Everybody enjoyed watching him ride around on his butt. He was something of an honored guest in many stores. They gave him alms willingly, without any complaints! He was doing very well, may the Evil Eye not harm him. When I asked about his wife, he answered with a little smile:

" '*Oy*, did Glupsk give me a fine wife! Did you ever hear of a cholera wife that turned out to be good? She should have died from the cholera before she became my wife. Her lower lip was missing, but that didn't keep her mouth from working, screaming, making noise all day long, grinding away like a mill, worse than a woman with two healthy lips.'

"I said to myself, 'There's no defense against a wife. If she is a scourge, she will scream even if she is missing a lip or a nose. She will fall upon you blindly even if she has no eyes.' I told Yontl about my wife and what I had to put up with.

" 'Don't be a fool!' he said. 'Do what I did. Spit at her and let it end at that. Let her go to the devil!'

" 'What do you mean, Yontl, spit at her? What about a divorce? I am a Jew and must be married.'

" 'Oho! You must be married?' Yontl looked at me with a laugh. 'You're really from Glupsk, upon my word! Fishke, listen to me. Stay here in Odessa a while and then we'll see.'

187

"After this, I used to meet Yontl often. I went all over Odessa with him, he on his butt and I on my lame legs. Yontl took it into his head to make me admire his Odessa. He showed me the beautiful streets and boasted about the beautiful houses, as if they belonged to him and gave him profit. Every time he showed me something, he looked at me with pride and snorted with pleasure, as though this wealthy house or that pretty street made him more important in my eyes. He would poke me and say, 'Nu, Fishke! What do you say about my Odessa? Maybe in your Glupsk you have something like this, eh?'

" 'Listen to me, Yontl!' I said to him one day when my sides were sore from his poking. He was showing me the Boulevard in the distance. Great crowds were strolling along it and I saw that he was unwilling to go up any closer. 'What do you want me to say, Yontl? Odessa is a beautiful city, but it's a pity that there are no *mentshen* here! Tell me yourself, Yontl, are those people out there on the Boulevard *mentshen*? Just look at the men holding the ladies' hands! It's a sin just to look! Jews with shaven faces! Jewish women with their own hair—sweeping the street with their long trailing dresses which are cut so low in front that you can see their bosoms. *Feh*, it's disgusting, as I am a Jew! *Ach*, if we could bring our Jews from Glupsk here! Then this would be a city, a Jewish city, with Jewish customs, and things would be as they should be.'

"Yontl moved along with me and said nothing. What could he say? On the way, two well-dressed gentlemen came toward us, Frenchmen, and Yontl stretched out his hand. One of them stopped to talk to him for a minute and gave him some money.

" 'Do you know, Fishke, who they are?' Yontl asked

188

with pride, his eyes shining with pleasure. 'The one who gave me money is the chief *melamed* in our *Talmud-Torah* here. An acquaintance of mine, do you understand? He cuts quite a figure, doesn't he?'

" 'May all my enemies look like that!' I spat. 'From the looks of my handsome *melamed,* I can imagine your so-called *Talmud-Torah* here. I ask you, Yontl, aren't you ashamed of yourself to say that this is good? No, no, Yontl! They've spoiled you here! You're just like them! Some *melamed!* Look at him and look at our Reb Hertzele Mazik in Glupsk, God forgive the comparison. There is a Jew for you! Why, all of Glupsk is full of Reb Hertzele Mazik. Who extols the dead at a funeral? He! Who makes the final arrangements for a wedding? He! Who recites psalms for the dead at the cemetery? He, again! When he goes from house to house every week to collect his fee for teaching the children, folks carry the money toward him! On *Simches-Torah* he runs to the wealthy houses with the little boys from the *Talmud-Torah* to say prayers in honor of the rich. When he cries, 'Holy sheep!' the little boys answer, 'Baa, ba-a-a!' It's something to see. And your Frenchman? What would he look like with his shaven face, reciting psalms? What would he look like extolling the dead at a funeral or saying prayers in honor of the rich?'

" 'But you're making a terrible mistake!' Yontl broke in. 'This *melamed* never does any such things and doesn't even know the first thing about them.'

" 'What do you mean, he doesn't do such things?' I asked in wonder.

" '*Sha, sha,* Fishke!' Yontl tried to calm me. 'He buries them, but in a different way. It's all right, the local gentlemen are satisfied—'

189

" '*Feh, feh, feh!*' I cried, stopping my ears. But Yontl wouldn't leave off and asked:

" 'And do you know who the second gentleman is? He is quite a man, a politician here in the city just like Aaron-Yossl Stillwhistler back in Glupsk!'

" '*Feh, feh!*' I shouted so angrily that several passers turned and looked. 'You call him a man, Yontl? Like our Reb Aaron-Yossl? At least you should add: forgive the comparison! Reb Aaron-Yossl is a Jew with a beard and with prayer curls! Jewishness is written all over him. He keeps Jewish money in trust: money willed for philanthropy, money belonging to the societies, and all sorts of other moneys. No one even asks him for a receipt, his word is good enough. When he takes money, he knows he is taking it and probably knows what to do with it. You can rely on him for that! And your man here? Who would want to trust him and for what? For his Jewishness? For his shaven prayer curls?'

" 'Just for his word, Fishke! Believe me!' Yontl insisted. 'With or without prayer curls, it makes no difference, as I am a Jew!'

" '*Ett!*' I said. 'What are you trying to prove to me? All right, I'll grant you that maybe his word can be trusted. But how could you let a person like that conduct a *Sandek*? Oh, he would do a fine job, I'm sure! *Feh!* It would be a joke! No wonder people say that you can see the flames of hell forty versts around Odessa! There must be some truth to it.

" 'Still,' Yontl answered bitingly, 'I'd rather be here in hell than back in that Garden of Eden of yours—Glupsk!'

"Yontl seemed altogether different to me now. Odessa had spoiled him and we argued very often. What he thought was good, I thought was bad, and what I thought was good, he thought was bad. We couldn't agree, for example, about the Big Synagogue in Odessa, or about the rabbi or the cantor there. A cantor, indeed! He sat in a booth while a chorus sang the prayers! He did nothing at all. You wouldn't catch him sticking his finger down his throat or pulling on his cheek like our Reb Jerechmiel Weepsister, who shouted in low register, then skipped to a few piercing notes like pistol shots, then back to the thick strings again, shifting the words up and down the scale, breaking into a thin falsetto for a sweet little Rumanian shepherd song with which he tried to soften the Lord of Nations: 'Oy, tatenyoo, dear Father! Oy vay, woe is me, woe!' Reb Jerechmiel put his heart and soul into his singing and was soaking wet by the time he reached 'Who is Blessed.' But the cantor here? Did he work like that? God forbid! He hardly did a thing. As soon as he sang a note, the chorus caught up the cue and dished it out on a little platter, carried it up and down, mixed it with kasha and poppy seeds! That's what they called 'services' here! And where was the Rumanian shepherd song? And where was the appeal to the Lord of Nations? Instead they made a fuss over an unimportant little prayer, 'There are none like unto Thee.' They worked it to death—a joke, as I'm a Jew! And what else? They held up the Torah and danced around the synagogue with it! Did you ever hear of anyone dancing with the Torah on Shabbes just like on Simches-Torah? Who ever heard of anything like that?

"Then you might ask, 'And where was the rabbi? How could he permit such things to go on?' That was the whole trouble! The rabbi himself led the dance in a French suit with a trimmed beard! *Feh!* And Yontl didn't mind at all!

" '*G'vald,* Yontl!' I exclaimed. 'Yontl, what have they done to you? Have you gone out of your mind or did you lose your senses? How can you stand such shamelessness? *G'vald,* the devil take your father's father!'

"And he grinned at me! He beamed with pride and said: 'Fishke, you're a fool! You can't even tell the difference between good and bad. How can anyone argue with you?'

"I saw that it was a lost cause. Yontl was stubborn. I knew that I couldn't get anywhere with him, so I promised myself not to talk about it any more. From now on people could stand on their heads in Odessa and I wouldn't care a fig!

" 'Listen,' I said to Yontl one day. 'I'm not going to argue with you any more about Odessa and its ways. You're a stubborn mule and I won't get anywhere with you. Let's talk about more important things! I need your advice— what's going to become of me? I'm sick of this begging from door to door. There are plenty of beggars without me. They cover this place like a horde of locusts and will soon cover the whole world. It would be better if I had some business or a trade. Tell me, what should I do?'

" 'Running an office is not for you,' answered Yontl. 'A store or shop is also no good. I don't know, why don't you tell me?'

" 'Don't laugh, Yontl,' I said. 'Talk sense. Jews do lots of other things besides running offices or stores or shops.'

" 'Oh, of course!' Yontl agreed. 'Like collecting the meat tax, for example, or keeping the treasury of a charity society, or collecting funds for Meyer Bel-Hannes' *Tal-*

" '*Nu*, Fishke?' Yontl asked with a little smile when I returned. 'Did you see any of the bathhouses here?'

" '*Ett*,' I answered without enthusiasm. 'There's nothing to talk about, really. Everything here is topsy-turvy. It's as if they were trying to make fun of the world. Your Odessa is not for me.'

XXIV

"I WAS NOT HAPPY IN ODESSA, BUT I HAD TO REMAIN THERE
through the winter. I couldn't have started out on the
road barefoot and naked in the middle of the winter all
alone in a strange part of the country. But as soon as the
bright sun made her warmth felt and the odors of summer
filled the air, something started pecking at me and
wouldn't let me sit still. There was a time when summer
made no difference to me. Just summer. Nothing special!
It was warm; the days were long and clear; it was green
all around. It felt good. The cows went to pasture. There
was more milk and a little sour cream. Also, I could eat
my bread with a green onion, some garlic, a fresh radish
or a cucumber. For a poor Jew, this changed a meal into
a feast.

"But this time summer was something special for me.
I don't know how to say it, but this summer spoke to me
with real words and filled my heart with desire. Everything reminded me of her, my dear hunchback. Each
little blade of grass, each little green tree, each trill of a
songbird—they all spoke to me and brought me regards
from her. I could see it all so clearly: how she had sat
with me, how she had looked, how she had laughed and
cried and poured out her bitter heart. My blood bubbled.
I fell into a sweet melancholy and something drew me,
drew me yonder, far away. Was it this particular summer? Did I catch some disease, some fever which made
me weak? I don't know. All I know is that I seemed to

197

be melting away like a candle. I was not the same as before.

" 'Fishke, are you sick?' Yontl asked me once after looking at me. 'Your face looks so thin. Does something hurt you?'

" '*Ett*, it's nothing,' I answered while I pressed my hands against my chest.

" 'Oh, it's your heart?' Yontl asked. 'There's a good medicine for that. Dip a piece of bread in salt and eat it on an empty stomach.'

" 'I have enough salt on my wounds already,' I answered with a sigh. 'I feel as if something is pressing on my heart. It presses and doesn't let me sit still.'

" 'Now I understand,' Yontl said with a little smile. 'It's your Glupsk that's doing it; Glupsk is calling you back. Back to where the stinkweed blooms, where poverty whistles in through the windows and garlic and onions perfume the air. Don't be ashamed, Fishke. Go back to where you'll feel at home again.'

"A few days later, I parted with Yontl and set out for home on foot.

"I had one thought on my mind and one feeling in my heart: she! Where was she, where could she be now? How was she getting along, poor dear, without me? And my feet moved along, by themselves somehow, slowly but surely on the road to Glupsk. I passed through towns and villages, and everywhere I went my eyes searched and searched—maybe I would meet her. I don't know how many Jewish towns I passed through, but the closer I came to Glupsk, the lighter my heart felt. It was a pleasure to be among our kind of Jews again. Their way of talking, the way they lived, their customs did my heart good. I felt that I was really back home among my own people. The Jews in our part of the country are so down to earth! No ceremonies, no fuss or bother, they just don't care about all the new-fangled ideas. If you feel like it, you can talk loud, shout at the top of your lungs, do as you please, just as God commanded. Whose affair is it if it's in place or out of place, if it's proper or not? If someone doesn't like it, let him close his eyes and stop his ears! I began to feel stronger. I calmed down, thought about Glupsk, about the stone bathhouse, and hoped that His Blessed Name would provide for me.

"One beautiful morning, I happened to be walking in wheatfields and cornfields and came up to a dense forest. I walked into it a ways, threw down my pack and took off my coat. I stretched out under a tree among some tall bushes whose big broad leaves hid me from sight. Well, what was there to worry about? It was a forest like any other forest with trees like any other trees and bushes like any other bushes. The songbirds were songbirds and I—I was Fishke and might just as well take a little nap and rest up from my journey. I stretched, yawned, closed my eyes—but listen to this dream. . . .

"I imagined I heard noises: footsteps and the snapping of dry branches. I pricked up my ears and listened with closed eyes. The rustling became louder and the footsteps nearer. I began to worry and wanted to open my eyes, but I couldn't. I lay like a log and couldn't move, I was so tired. The footsteps seemed to move away. I calmed down and fell asleep. It felt so sweet, so good. I heard a soft, sad tune. There was something familiar about it. The tune went through my whole body and made me dizzy. I felt like crying and laughing at the same time. Just like a bride and groom laugh and cry before they go under the *chupeh*—at one and the same time—like a summer shower while the sun is shining.

"Suddenly, someone pulled my hair and screamed. I jumped up quickly and spread the broad leaves apart. I saw a pot full of big red berries lying on its side near me. Not far away a woman sat on the ground, looking around fearfully. I soon understood what had happened. She must have been gathering berries here. Her mind was occupied with her search and she had been humming busily to herself. She must have touched my hair and that scared her. I picked up the pot and called to her in a friendly way: 'Everything's all right!' But as soon as I came closer, the pot slid out of my hands, a shout escaped from my lips and my feet froze in their tracks. A minute later, we were squeezing each other's hands and looking into each other's eyes, my dear hunchback and I.

"This was no dream! I was awake. I looked around. I was in a thick forest of big trees. Way up on the highest branches, little birds hopped up and down. They trilled and whistled and shared our happiness. We were both so happy. We laughed through our tears. We marveled at finding each other here and couldn't stop talking and telling each other about what we had been through during the last year.

"She told me about the torments she had had to suffer since the band had abandoned me last year. It was all the bastard's doing. He did not want my wife to divorce me. He was afraid that she might insist that he marry her. He wanted a blind woman but not a blind wife. He was glad to make love to her and make money with her, but let someone else take care of her. He also wanted to get even with me by keeping me from being free. My friend-

ship with the hunchbacked girl was like a knife in his breast. He was ready to do anything to keep it from going any further. As soon as he was rid of me, he took my wife in hand and began to teach her who was master. He knew that it was impossible for her to escape his clutches now. What could a blind woman do by herself? He finally became sick and tired of her and gave her to the little old man. She had to play the part and go begging with him from house to house like I used to do. The bastard ground her under his heel. He beat her without mercy, while the little old man had his own methods of teaching her. In a short time, she began to look like an old woman.

"The band had been roaming the countryside all year and visited many towns. This morning, they had stopped here in the forest to rest. She had an urge to go picking berries and suddenly—she said with a little smile—she stumbled on a very good one: me.

"I told her in turn where I had been during the year and how I had chanced to stop there that morning on my way to Glupsk. We decided never to part again. We would do everything we could to talk my wife into giving me a divorce. If, God forbid, she refused, we would run away from the band anyway and hope for the best. As we sat there, enjoying each other's company, we heard someone shout 'A-ha!' somewhere deep in the woods.

" 'That's one of them calling,' my hunchback explained. 'They're looking for me.'

"A little later, one of them came by. I recognized him. He looked at me crookedly and, laughing, rushed back in a hurry to announce the good news. We got up also and, taking our time, slowly set off for the camp. Behind a little inn, a crumbling ruin, I recognized a line of familiar-looking vans stretching back into the woods. Beyond the vans, in a clearing, burned a merry fire. The whole band was gathered around it.

"My first *sholem-aleichem* came from the bastard, who sounded off in a loud voice: 'A-a-a-h! A dear guest, indeed! How do you do? I was beginning to miss you, Reb Fish!'

"And soon the air was filled with shouts: 'Look who's here! Come, let's welcome the Magnate!' And from all sides, wild greetings came down on me together with blows and pinches, so that I lost my cap. I covered my head with the hem of my coat and bent down to find it while they beat me without stopping. Just then, my wife came running all out of breath and full of joy.

"'Where is he, my dear one? Where, where's my Fishke?!'

"Her joy hurt more than all the pinches and blows put together. 'Her joy won't help me get a divorce from her,' I thought. 'I'd be better off if she hated me like the others here do!' But she hung around my neck and called to her own dear Fishke. I felt very bad to see her looking this way—a blind, dried-up, weak, old woman! Where was her plumpness, her health, her chubby cheeks and mouth? I had to force myself to ask her, for old times' sake, 'How are you, Bassia?'

"'Oh, you were right, Fishke, when you used to say that in Glupsk we both, blessed be His Name, had a reputation. People knew me there and respected me!' my wife declared in a loud voice so that everybody would hear. She looked around proudly, like a fallen magnate talking about the wealth he had had years ago. She sighed deeply and continued: 'We've wandered long enough. Let's go home, lead me home! Fishke, back to our city, to our houses, to our rich folks!'

"Her talk made me feel nauseous. I didn't expect such a greeting from her and I made a face. The bastard made an ugly face too, thinking that I wanted to rob him of his goods and ruin his trade. But my thoughts were quite different: 'She's all yours, if you want her. I forgive you with all my heart—take her!'

"He must have been raging with fury. He glared at me until his eyes became bloodshot. Then he got up with a growl and marched away angrily.

"The women and girls of this fine crowd were busy around the fire, pushing pots in, pulling them out, baking potatoes. Some of the younger fellows hung around, fooling with them and teasing them, sneaking in a slap here and there, or stealing a quiet pinch—all accompanied by wisecracks. The women acted angry. They scolded and cursed but giggled and laughed at the same time. They let themselves be caught like hens by the barnyard rooster when he spreads his wings, and lovingly pecks their heads.

"The other beggars were spread all over the woods. One lay on his belly snoring for all he was worth. Another one was busy patching an old robe. A third one was scratching himself with such a serious expression on his face that it looked like he was hunting for gold. Still others were wrestling, trying to see who was stronger. Life went on at its merry pace here!

"My wife clung to me and wouldn't let go—one body and one soul. She talked a blue streak, lamented her bitter lot, told me how she had suffered. She wanted only one thing now—that I should take her away from here and live with her, as God had commanded, to the end of our ordained years. I said one word for every ten of hers and looked for a way to get out of her clutches. When she finally ran out of talk, I managed to squirm out of her grip and catch my breath. I looked for my dear hunchback and quietly went off with her. Things looked bad for us. There was no sense in bringing up the subject of a divorce. My wife wouldn't even listen. She would snort and toss her head. I couldn't stay here with the band of thieves either. It meant selling myself to the devil again. It meant playing the bear for them again. What could I do?

"We puzzled over this for a while. Finally we decided that the only choice was to run away. Since the band was going to spend the night here, this night here in the woods was the time and place to do it. As we sat together thinking over our plan, the bastard appeared in the distance with a pair of horses. 'Let's not wait,' said my hunchback, 'until he comes closer. It won't do any good for him to see us sitting together. Let's separate while there is still time.'

"She went off to one side and I to the other.

"The bastard was very busy and whispered all the while to the little old man, his right-hand man. I stayed out of the bastard's sight. While the other beggars worked and fooled with each other, my hunchback came up to me and whispered in my ear that the bastard wanted to move on before sundown. That pair of horses was stolen and he was in a hurry to get out of this neighborhood. All our work, our whole plan, collapsed like a house of cards. I stood helpless and didn't know what to do next. My heart felt as if it was pressed in a vise. My head spun so that I could hardly stand on my feet. My hunchback looked at me with great pity. Her eyes burned like coals of fire and her face was aflame. She thought for a while and said to me with a quivering voice:

205

" 'Fishke! A little later, try to be in that little ruined inn, in the attic. Do you understand?'

" 'I understand, I understand!' I almost shouted. 'And you'll come there later?'

" 'Yes, *sha!*' she said, nodding. 'But it must be done quietly. Do you hear?'

"I didn't think it necessary to say good-bye to my wife. I pitied her, but it was her own fault. She was the first to make a crack in our marriage and the crack grew wider and wider. Now it was all over. What could I do? Just as the sky and the earth will never meet, so she and I couldn't think of ever coming together again. That's why I didn't bother saying good-bye to her, and quietly slipped away to the little inn.

"You can imagine how I felt when I went into the ruined little inn. After so much trouble, so many heartaches, God was going to unite me with my dear hunchback in a crumbling hut. Here our lot would be changed. From now on we would lead a new life! I had no trouble climbing into the attic. The hut was low and the rear wall so fallen to pieces that the roof almost touched the ground. The ceiling was full of cracks so that I could look down from the attic into the room below. I sat down in a corner and waited. My heart pounded like a hammer. Each minute seemed like a year to me. I froze stiff at every sound: the least motion of a straw and I thought it was a step, that she was coming; the softest breeze, and I thought it was she calling my name. Suddenly I heard a voice in the room below. The thought that it was she, that she was here, that soon, soon we would both be free made me shake like a leaf. I felt hot and cold at the same time. I would have called out but my voice choked and my tongue wouldn't move. At this moment I heard someone call my

206

name very clearly. I looked through a crack and whom did I see? The bastard and the little old man!

" 'You take care of your piece of goods,' said the bastard. 'Make sure that the blind witch doesn't slip. You understand?'

" 'Don't worry!' answered the little old man. 'I've done my part. I just hope she doesn't die on me. The old nag is lying there like dead and doesn't move, I gave her such a beating!'

" 'And that lame good-for-nothing,' said the bastard, 'belongs to me! I can't stand the sight of his ugly mug— that's how much I hate him. I'll fix him, don't you worry! I've got an old score to settle with him.'

"My blood froze in my veins when I heard these terrible words.

" 'It seems,' the old man commented, 'that your stolen horses belong to Jews. They're dried up, beaten, sick, with crooked spines, and thin necks like birds, and piles too. Fine creatures indeed, just like their owners.'

" 'May your tongue rot, you old buzzard!' the bastard cursed. 'You'd better look around, you old dog, and see if you can't sniff out some old clothes that we can use. There might be some up in the attic. After all, this was an inn once upon a time.'

"I broke out in a cold sweat. I felt so sick, I thought I'd die. My lame leg began to tremble badly and knocked against the floor. The two fine gentlemen looked up and gaped at the ceiling for a while. Then they both exclaimed together:

" 'There's dust falling from the ceiling! We'd better take a look.'

"My head spun, my ears rang, I saw spots before my eyes and felt as though I was flying through the air.

"Yes, through the air. A pair of iron hands grabbed me and flung me down from the attic to the floor below. Someone greeted me with a loud 'Welcome!' and a sneer: 'Well, if it isn't Reb Fish!' I looked up and saw the bastard glaring down at me. His face was terrible to see— it was the face of a cat ready to choke a captured mouse. The little old man wasn't there any more. He had disappeared, leaving me to face the bastard alone.

" '*Nu*, confess your sins, you carrion!' said the bastard. 'What I should have done to you back there in the cellar, I'll do now. Don't you worry, Feibushke doesn't forget!'

"I fell at his feet and begged him, as I would have begged a murderer, to grant me my life. It was no use. He took out a knife, held it before my eyes, and watched gleefully how I shivered and shook. I tried to convince him that if he let me go, he would go to heaven after he died. I even offered him my share of Paradise. I tried everything possible. He glared at me and said nothing. I began to threaten him with God's vengeance, with the fires of hell, with the price he'd pay for shedding innocent blood. He bit his lip, raised the knife—and just as the blade was at my throat, someone behind him snatched it from his hand with a cry that wasn't human: 'No, no! You won't dare!'

"He looked around, frightened. It was the hunchbacked girl!

" 'Get out of here, you tramp!' he shouted wildly as soon as he had recovered. 'Get out, or—'

" 'No, no! I will not get out of here! I'd rather die here together with him,' my hunchback shouted back hotly and fell down before him, crying bitter tears, begging for mercy, caressing him so that he would let me go. She too promised him her share of Paradise. The bastard flung her away from himself like a little ball. He cursed and swore for all he was worth. When he finally calmed down a little, he turned to me and said:

" 'It's too bad that I don't have you here alone, you hunk of garbage. You can thank your filthy luck, you stinking carrion, that I haven't crushed you like a louse between my fingers! But I won't let you off so easy!'

"He took the rope from around his waist and tied my hands and feet, saying: 'Lie here quietly, you dog! Don't even let me hear a whimper from you! Lie here until you croak! But remember, you good-for-nothing, if, by some miracle, you get out of this, if some mother's mother of yours should rise from her grave to help you, keep out of my way forever. Don't let me ever lay an eye on you again, because if I do . . . kh—kh—kh——k!' And he passed his finger across his throat to show me what he meant.

"When he was done with me, he turned to my hunchback, who was sobbing on the floor.

" 'Ah, you tramp, you!' the bastard growled, shoving her, poor thing, with his foot. 'I understand everything, don't you worry! You two had a private arrangement—a wedding without musicians, up there in the attic. A fine little girl you are. I know all about it. But with me she acts as pure as a rabbi's wife. From now on, I'll know better how to deal with you, you tramp!'

"He seized her and turned to me: 'Remember what I said, you dog!' Then he disappeared with her.

"Can I tell you how I suffered? The torments of hell can't be worse! I was not in hell—hell was in me. A wild, hellish fire burned within me. My hair stood on end. My scalp felt as though red-hot pins were pricking it, yet I couldn't cry out or even breathe too loud.

"A little later, I heard noises far away: the scraping of

wheels, people shouting, the sounds of moving. The band was leaving—the whole crowd of them, and with them, my heart, my dear, good, unfortunate hunchback, poor thing.

"For a long time I lay like a stupid sheep with all four legs tied. My eyes were filled with hot tears. The rope burned my skin and felt like a knife cutting me every time I moved. My throat was dry and I was dying for a drink. I thought I would pass out at any moment. Everything hurt so much that I began to scream in case someone was passing by. I figured that the band must be quite far away now. I shouted, I screamed, but it was no use. I might as well have shouted to the wall. My throat was raw and I was aching all over. It was harder and harder to yell. I had to rest more and more. I hardly had any strength left to cry out. I clung to life by a thin thread, and the Angel of Death, I was sure, had come to break that thread. It was my lot to die young, to leave my years unfulfilled. I collected the little strength left in me and shouted one last time—my last cry to the world about my unfortunate life.

"But God brought you to the rescue, Reb Alter! You came in a time of need and saved my life."

XXV

AS FISHKE FINISHED HIS SAD TALE, NIGHT FELL AND OUR
horses arrived at the green hill just before Glupsk. The
green hill of Glupsk is known almost all over the world.
There is an ancient folk song, sung by young and old,
about it. Mothers and wet-nurses soothe their crying
babes and rock them to sleep with it. My own mother, may
she thrive in Paradise, also used to sing me this song when
I was still in diapers:

> "Way up yon green hill
> Where the grass grows tall,
> A pair of Germans stand
> Their long whips in hand.
> Tall men two are they,
> But their pants are short,
> Our Father, our King . . ."

This used to be my favorite song. Somehow, my childish
mind imagined the green hill to be wondrously beautiful.
I used to think that it was not made of common soil like
the other hills around my town, but of some indescriba-
bly rare and delightful stuff—like Mount Olive or Mount
Lebanon—of the soil of the Land of Israel.

And the Germans! I imagined them to be a sort of out-
landish creature, may they pardon me, something in the
nature of cattle or oxen, like the legendary Wild Bull.
Their long whips whistled through the air and guarded
the approaches to Glupsk like the River *Sambatyon*

guards the approach to the home of the Little Red Jews. Anyone entering Glupsk must receive the lash. And, to tell the truth, everyone in Glupsk did have a beaten look.

In later years, when I had outgrown my children's shoes and had seen something of the world, I looked at things with different eyes and understood the true meaning of the little ditty. The green hill was really nothing more than an ordinary hill—not green, but muddy, full of ruts. And the Germans, tall men two, they were merely a hint at those gentlemen with long hands and sticky fingers who robbed the wagons and stole the goods of travelers to Glupsk. People who came to Glupsk for the first time generally took no special precautions. But the second time, they would become uneasy several versts before reaching the city. Their eyes began to search all around them to make sure that there were no strangers in their vans. Their fingers patted their bosom pockets and buttoned their coats from top to bottom to make sure that everything inside would remain there. All I am trying to say is that upon reaching the green hill, each of our senses, including our noses, became aware of the nearness of Glupsk. A little later, after we had looked around in all directions and checked the contents of our wagons, we remembered Fishke and saw him sitting quietly, poor fellow, downcast and drooping.

I began to cheer him up. I tried to raise his spirits with brave words. I sang the other half of the previously mentioned ditty, to put him in a good humor:

> "Our Father, our King
> My heart with joy does sing.
> We shall be tickled pink
> And wine by the bottle drink.

Of *kreplach* shall we eat our fill
But forget our beloved God?
That, we never will!"

"Stop worrying, Fishke. We must never forget our beloved God. He can help us."

"I only want to ask you one question, Reb Mendele!" Fishke exclaimed bitterly. "Why did He have to bring us together again, her and me, and then separate us so suddenly? Why did our luck suddenly smile on us only to make things blacker than ever before? It's almost like spite work! Oh, Lord of Nations, whom hast Thou punished? Two unfortunate, miserable cripples, who would have been far better off if they'd never been born! Their lives have been so bleak, so full of pain and torments!"

I made a pious face, shook my head and said: "*Ta, ta, ta!* You mustn't talk like that." I did not say this because it answered Fishke's cry of woe in any way, but rather because it has become a custom in the world. When misery forces someone to start asking embarrassing questions, you must chide him and slow him down with at least a *"Ta, ta, ta!"* Having thus satisfied tradition, I went on to speak like a human being.

"Tell me, Fishke, what is the girl's name? Until now, you've only called her the hunchbacked girl, or 'my dear hunchback.' Now I'd like to know her name."

"What for, Reb Mendele?" Fishke looked at me in wonder. "Why do you want to know, please? Why bandy a girl's name about in vain?"

"Don't you understand, silly fellow," I answered, "that I might be able to help you if I know it? In my travels, it just might happen that I should come across a clue, a hint.

213

Tell me her name. Don't worry about it! It's very possible, you understand, that you may recover your loss. Let me be your emissary!"

"Bayleh is her name," Fishke burst out all at once. "Her name is Bayleh!"

Suddenly, I heard a loud groan and a thud, as if something had fallen down. I turned around in fright and saw my Reb Alter stretched out in the wagon, gasping for breath and white as a sheet.

"What is it, Reb Alter?" I asked. "You don't feel well? Maybe you'd like some brandy?"

"*Beh!*" Alter answered and, with an effort, sat up again.

"Tell me, Fishke!" I continued when I was sure that Alter was in no danger: "do you also know what was her mother's name and where she is from?"

"Yes," Fishke answered. "My hunchback told me that her mother's name was Elkeh. She remembered that her mother and father were divorced in Tuneyadevkeh. Her mother used to talk about it whenever she lost her temper with the miserable child."

"Divorced in Tuneyadevkeh?" I wondered. "Who could have been her husband there—that monster of monsters, with a heart of stone, who cast off his child and made her life miserable? Eh, Reb Alter, it's your town. Who could it have been?"

Alter sat there more dead than alive. His bulging eyes rolled wildly. My heart sank when I saw him gasping for breath.

"His name was . . ." Fishke rubbed his forehead in an effort to recall the name. "His name, his name, I think . . . wait a minute—"

"Alter is his name!" Alter screamed and again fell down in the wagon.

214

"Yes, yes, that's it!" Fishke exclaimed, looking at Alter without understanding the meaning of his screaming. "And he had another name—Yaknehoz. Her mother used to pinch her cruelly and call her 'Yaknehoz's daughter' or 'Lady Yaknehoz,' especially after she'd had a lot of trouble or lost a job."

By now everything was crystal-clear to me and I sat there as if I had been doused with a pail of cold water.

Alter sobbed and beat his breast with his fist, crying, "Verily, I have sinned! I have ruined her life. She was right, poor thing, with her little song:

'My father used to hate me . . .'

That's why the wrath of God has descended upon me. That's why my luck is bad no matter what I do. Everything is *shlimmazel.* . . ."

I began to reassure Reb Alter for pity's sake. I tried to soothe him and minimize his sins: he was, after all, no more than flesh and blood. The Evil Genius was very powerful among us sinners. Even great *tsadikim* have succumbed in these matters and have not been able to overcome the Evil Genius in regards to women and marriage. Many of our ancestors, *tsadikim,* lay under their wives' heels, fulfilled their wives' commands and drove away their own children by another marriage.

For Fishke, this whole scene was crazy. He stared at us in surprise, looked first at Alter and then at me and didn't know what to do next.

In the meanwhile, night fell. The stars twinkled, winked down to us from the heavens with their shimmering faces, as though they would have liked to take part in our conversation. At the edge of the sky, a big moon, as red as fire, began to rise out of the earth. It almost seemed to be looking directly at us. All the inhabitants of the realms above were watching and waiting for the end of the story. Suddenly, my Alter sat bolt upright, lifted his eyes toward the heavens and spoke with earnestness:

"I swear by Him who lives eternally, that I shall not return home to my wife and children, that I will not marry off my eldest daughter before I find my unfortunate child! Heaven and earth are my witnesses! I am leaving immediately and woe to him who stands in my way."

Fishke fell on Alter's neck, embraced him and kissed him without words. Then, with tears in his voice, he exclaimed: "*G'vald,* save her, save her!"

My Alter swiftly jumped from my wagon, climbed up on his, and waving good-bye to us, turned around, lashed his nag and drove off. Fishke and I watched him for a while without saying a word. Then I glanced up at the sky. The moon and stars were going their way, but they looked different than before. They were not as friendly. They had become distant and haughty. My heart grew sad and heavy.

I lashed my eagle so as to remind him that he still had a job to do pulling the wagon. It was late at night when we rolled into the rutted streets of Glupsk. The roar and rumble of our wheels announced to the inhabitants:

"Attention! Be it known that two new Jews have arrived in the city of Glupsk!"

GLOSSARY

Ben Zochor—a family gathering to celebrate the birth of a boy. The celebration takes place on the first Friday evening after his birth.

Betsa—literally, an egg. This is the name of a tractate in the *Gemara* which begins by considering the propriety of eating an egg that was laid on a Holy Day.

briss—a contraction of *briss mila*—circumcision.

chalah—a twisted white bread eaten on the Sabbath and holidays.

Chanukah—the Feast of the Dedication commemorating the liberation of the Temple in Jerusalem from the Syrians and Greeks.

chappers—snatchers. Men who snatched poor Jewish children and orphans off the street to serve in the Tsar's army, in lieu of the children of rich families.

cheder—the religious elementary school conducted by a *melamed,* usually in his own house.

chupeh—the bridal canopy. The four poles signify the four corners of the world. A blue cloth, symbolic of the heavens, is supported by the poles.

dybbuk—a ghost or spirit which enters and takes possession of a person's body.

Esau—Jacob's brother—the hunter, the outdoor man, the unrefined man—often used to denote a non-Jew in a derisive manner.

esrog—a citrus fruit similar to a lemon; one of the four plants used during the Feast of Weeks (*Shevuoth*).

farfel—small pieces of dough, either cooked or uncooked.

Gemara—the Commentaries of the *Talmud*.

Golem of Reb Laib Sarah's—Rabbi Laib Sarah's was a Polish Chassidic Rabbi. His magical power was the subject of many popular legends. Like other *tsadikim*, he had the power to create a *Golem*, a dead body of clay into which he instilled life by incanting the proper words. Only the *tsadik* could deprive the *Golem* of his life.

g'vald—a cry of distress: "Help!"

Haggadah—the order of the home services at the *seder* on Passover night.

House of Study—translation of *Bess-Hamedresh*, an edifice used both for praying and studying the *Torah* as distinguished from a *Shul* or *Bess-Haknessess* (synagogue) which was used exclusively for praying. Every Jewish town had a House of Study near its synagogue. The House of Study often served as a meeting house for discussing communal and worldly affairs.

kadish—a memorial prayer recited over the grave of the dead and on the anniversary of death each year.

Kahal—the seat of administration of whatever autonomy was granted to the Jewish community by the Tsar.

kasha—porridge, frequently made of whole buckwheat.

kiddush—benediction or sanctification of *Shabbes* and festivals; pronounced over a cup of wine.

kishka—section of intestine stuffed with flour and chicken fat.

knaydlech—dumplings made of matzo-meal with the addition of melted goose or chicken fat.

kugl—a pudding made of flour and fat, often eaten on *Shabbes*.

lekech—a form of honeycake, often served with wine on a festive occasion.

Megillah—literally, a scroll; the name of a tractate of the *Talmud*.

melamed—a teacher of young children. See *cheder*.

mentsh—this word involves a whole philosophy of life. The meaning of *mentsh* is a human being in the moral and ethical sense; not merely a person, but a person with worth and dignity, one who can be respected. *Mentshen* is the plural form.

Mezuzah—a piece of parchment containing 22 lines from Deuteronomy. It is rolled up in a wooden, metal, or glass cylinder and attached to the doorpost of Jewish homes. It is kissed upon entering and leaving the house.

milchikeh—Jewish religious dietary laws distinguish between two chief types of food: the *milchikeh* (dairy) and the *flayshikeh* (meat) which may not be eaten together.

mitzvah—an act performed as prescribed by Jewish religion or law or in the interest of fellow Jews; hence, a good deed.

Purim—the Feast of Lots. This joyful holiday symbolizes the victory of the Jews over their persecutors.

rebbe—here used as a term synonymous with *melamed*.

rebitsin—literally, the rabbi's wife; often sarcastically applied to a woman who gives herself airs.

Rosh-Chodesh—literally, the first day of the month. The first day of each month is a festive occasion in the Jewish religion. Special prayers are said, particularly in benediction of the new moon.

Sambatyon—according to a Jewish legend, the ten lost tribes of Israel live in a distant land, at the end of the world, behind the high Dark Mountains and the River Sambatyon. This river rages and roars, spewing huge boulders which make it impossible to cross. According to other legends, the inhabitants of that distant land are called the "Little Red Jews."

Sandek—the godfather of a boy; the *Sandek* holds the baby boy on his knee for circumcision.

seder—the home service and meal on several nights during the week of Passover.

Shabbes—literally, the Sabbath. The festivity of the Jewish *Shabbes* on which, for one day, the man of the house is king and his wife is queen is quite different from the spirit of somberness which is sometimes associated with the non-Jewish Sabbath.

shammes—the attendant in a synagogue.

shlimmazel—an unlucky person whose life is a series of misfortunes. The word often has an amusing connotation.

shofar—a ram's horn which is blown in the synagogue on *Yom Kippur*, the Day of Atonement, and *Rosh-Hashana*, the first day of the new year.

sidra—the portion of the Pentateuch (*Chumosh*) which is read at the services on *Shabbes*.

Simches-Torah—the festival of the Rejoicing of the Torah.

talles—a prayer shawl.

Tammuz—the fourth month of the Jewish calendar. It corresponds to June-July.

techina—a prayer book of supplication for women, containing lachrymose comments on various aspects of daily life.

tefillin—phylacteries. The tefillin consist of two leather boxes containing passages from the Pentateuch. One box is worn on the head and the other is strapped to the left arm while the appropriate prayers are recited.

Tisha B'ov—the ninth day in the month of Ab; a fast day commemorating the destruction of the first and second temples.

tsadik—literally, a righteous man. In Chassidic and Cabbalistic lore, the *tsadik* plays an important role. The legends state that in each generation there are 36 *tsadikim* whose identity is secret and who are outwardly simple people—but the world rests on their righteousness. They are often endowed with magical powers.

Yaknehoz—this odd nickname of Alter's is composed of the first letters of several words: *ya*, for wine; *k*, for *kiddush*; *ne*, for candle; *ha*, for *Havdalah*, which is a *Shabbes* benediction; and *z*, for time. These are an indication of the wares he handled, namely goods serving the religious needs of the people and yielding but little income. There is a saying: "He sells *yaknehoz*," meaning useless, profitless items.